Psychic Man vs. Omnipotent Government

There was a proposal before the U.S. Senate—a proposal to build a secret underground complex to house the nation's defense facilities in the event of nuclear holocaust.

But the complex was to have another purpose as well, a purpose only a handful of men were entrusted to know: it would be a city designed to protect the nation's "elite" in time of crisis, leaving the "unqualified" to fend for themselves. A city that would serve as a testing ground for scientists to experiment with human mind control. A city that would destroy America—unless Peter Roos, brother of the project's chief sponsor, could find a way to stop it!

"An entertaining psychological thriller!"
—*Los Angeles Times*

Books by Kate Wilhelm

City of Cain
The Clewiston Test
Fault Lines
Juniper Time
Margaret and I
A Sense of Shadow
Where Late the Sweet Birds Sang

Published by TIMESCAPE BOOKS

KATE WILHELM
CITY OF CAIN

A TIMESCAPE BOOK
PUBLISHED BY POCKET BOOKS NEW YORK

The italicized sentence on page 101 is taken from *Jealousy*, by
Alain Robbe-Grillet. Copyright © 1965 by Grove Press, Inc.

POCKET BOOKS, a Simon & Schuster division of
GULF & WESTERN CORPORATION
1230 Avenue of the Americas, New York, N.Y. 10020

Published by arrangement with Little, Brown and Company
Library of Congress Catalog Card Number: 73-15818

ISBN: 0-671-44705-X

First Pocket Books printing July, 1978

10 9 8 7 6 5 4 3 2

POCKET and colophon are registered trademarks
of Simon & Schuster.

Printed in the U.S.A.

To all the friends I have made through Milford and Clarion, in gratitude for what they have taught me. With a special thanks to C. Davis Belcher, M.D.

CITY OF CAIN

Chapter 1

Toward dawn Peter's eyes started to burn. He rubbed them lightly, tried to focus on the book again, finally gave it up and turned off the light. The world was done in many shades of black, his room the blackest of them all. The black of the oak tree took shape from the black of the sky, as if drawing from the lightening sky its darkness, making itself solid, making the air above it, beyond it, thin and translucent. There were dried leaves on the tree, endlessly whispering in an unknown tongue that seemed almost intelligible, tenaciously hanging on through winter storms, scorching sun, winds, rains. Dead, brown leaves, useless and mindless, also stubborn.

Peter heard the alarm clock down the hall, muted, faint through doors and walls and distance. Moments later there was Ed's deep voice, reassuringly vibrant even in the cold light of early morning, and Lillian's morning-shrill voice that would change throughout the day, to become almost sultry by night. Did she practice, forgetting only when sleep had dimmed even the most urgent needs? Soon voices of the girls were there. That morning only one of the girls got up; the other, Bobby, was recovering from a virus. Lying in bed, looking at the cool sky that hadn't turned to any color yet, but was like flawed milk glass, Peter listened to the morning noises in the house, not wanting to catch the words, unable not to hear them.

From down the hall, from the bathrooms, footsteps padding, thumping on stairs; water running, doors closing, slamming, a child's agony, or hilarity.

"Is he up yet?" Ed's voice.

"I don't think he got into bed before dawn. I was up to see about Bobby and I could hear him moving about."

"Let him sleep. How's Bobby?"

The oak branches changed color as the sky brightened behind them. Peter thought about gradual changes, and tried to watch change happen, and failed.

"Mother, isn't Bobby going to school again today?"

"No, dear. Why?"

"Her teacher said I should pick up her things, but I don't want to. I'm supposed to go to band practice, and I don't want to lug her books and notebook and everything else."

"All right. Don't worry about it."

"For God's sake..." Ed's voice again.

"What...?"

"A leak. Pryor has the story about Wednesday's executive hearings, complete with a list of the witnesses and quotes."

"How does he do it?" Then, two octaves higher, decibels louder: "Elaine, aren't you ready yet?"

The sky had turned clear blue, endless, and the oak tree had finished itself. Beautiful morning. Beautiful tree. How had it managed to escape the saw? Hadn't some tree surgeon spotted it back there, or the contractor, when he put in the new driveway? A gray squirrel raced up the oak, stopped to regard Peter with unreadable, unwavering eyes. Smartass squirrel, five days in a row he had fed it peanuts, and it still watched him as if it knew about men and shotguns.

"I don't care if it isn't the sweater you wanted, Elaine. You're going to make your father late if you don't hurry. Now come on."

The squirrel moved, gone in a blur of motion. The garage door opened, metal scraped metal, ending on a high, painful note; the car backed to the front of the old Georgian house. A horn sounded once, Ed's touch very light; front door opened, banged. A revved-up motor, gears engaging. Silence.

Peter's hands ached, and he realized he was clenching them.

He forced his fists to open, relax. He got up. Mrs. Haines, the housekeeper, would be there at nine, the maid soon after that, and if he was in the kitchen then, he would be in their way. He went down in robe and slippers.

"Morning, Peter, I guess we woke you up, didn't we? Sorry."

"Hi, Lil. No, I was awake." She was almost forty and looked it in the morning, but not later in the day, and never at night.

"Did you ever sleep?"

"A little, not much. It's all right. I don't seem to miss it." His fingers moved toward the spot on his scalp—the plug—that had been put there by doctors and he forced them instead to rub his beard. "Sorry about this. You mind if I show up unshaved for breakfast?"

"You know we don't. Can I...?"

She made the polite noise but didn't rise. She had folded the paper when he entered the breakfast room and held it, ready to reopen. Later she would speak of Ann Landers' column with amusement.

"I'll fix something," he said. "Bobby better this morning?"

"Oh, yes. Probably she could have gone to school today, but one more day at home won't hurt anything."

"If you have anything to do today, Lil, go on. I'll keep the princess quiet and content."

"How did you guess! I do have an author's tea at the library. If you're sure. I don't think she's really sick now. A two-day virus or something."

"Sure. Sure. She'll be okay. I'll read Kant to her."

Lil looked at him quickly, but he went on into the kitchen. "Has she had breakfast yet?" he called back.

"No. Said she wasn't hungry."

He whistled as he scrambled eggs and made toast, and the whistle was for Lil's benefit. If he wasn't cheerful she might try to help. He heated two plates, took a carton of milk, and orange juice, and assembled two breakfasts on a tray. Folding a towel over his arm, spreading another over the tray, he went through the dining room and up the stairs. "You'll spoil her to death," Lil said to his back. He nodded. He thought it strange that she didn't like for him to treat her children like people.

Outside Bobby's door he paused a moment listening.

She was reading. He could hear the pages rustle. He hit the door with his knee. "Madam, breakfast is served."

"Peter? Is that you?" Getting out of bed sounds, bare feet running across the floor. Door flung wide. "What have you got?"

"Madam, such familiarity with the servants is beneath your high station. Really!" He turned his head. "You're not even decent."

Bobby laughed and ran back to the bed. "Can I eat in bed, Peter? Can you prop the tray up for me in bed?"

He propped the tray and they ate their breakfasts. Bobby chatted continuously, and now and again Peter answered her questions or volunteered a comment. Behind her noises he heard the housekeeper arrive and ten minutes later, the maid Rita, Lillian on the telephone, then coming up the stairs, pausing at Bobby's door, going on to her own room, returning.

He promised to give Bobby a test in arithmetic later in the day, and to quiz her on spelling.

"Daddy says that you have to go to school too," she said. Her expression said she didn't believe it.

"He's wrong," Peter said. "What he meant was that he wishes I would go to school again. And if he were I, then he would go back to school. Or if I were he. Or me him, or whatever." Bobby laughed at his worried look.

"It's 'If he was me,'" she said.

"Thank you, madam."

"If you did go to school, what would you learn?"

"Not much."

"I'm learning a lot. Why wouldn't you learn a lot too?"

"Because I already learned a lot, pumpkin. I know more than anyone on earth. And that's why."

"I knew it! That's what I told Daddy. You are just going to stay here with us, aren't you?"

He heard Lil outside the door. Listening. He grinned at Bobby and made a face. She squealed, and Lil entered.

"Bobby, did you eat?"

She looked from the child to Peter sitting on the window seat, to the empty plates and the empty glasses.

"Dear, I have to go out in a little while, but Uncle Peter will be here, and Mrs. Haines."

"Okay," Bobby said.

Lil felt her forehead and Bobby tried to move away from her hand. "Can I get up now?"

"I guess so. But don't go outside and no roughhousing." Lil turned to Peter. "You don't have to stay with her all day, you know. I should have got her up and sent her to school this morning."

Late in the afternoon Bobby slept and Peter read and thought. They wanted him to get back to a normal life. He worried them. What they didn't tell him was what was a normal life. More school? Ed applied pressure now and then, not for anything as firm as a promise, rather an indication, a hint that Peter would be ready in the fall to go back for his doctorate.

It was the damnable insomnia, he thought. Too much time to think. And the thoughts went nowhere. Sometimes he thought that he was skirting something important, something too elusive to grasp, too important to let him be able to dismiss it along with the other amnesiac blanks that still seemed to make up most of his past. Sometimes when he tried to get inside his head, he managed to achieve peace for awhile. It never lasted.

Dinner. Bobby was at table with the family. She was a pixie with short, very curly hair, too curly, she said often, trying to brush it straight. Elaine, a young lady of twelve now, experimented with lipstick and bras, tried not to be self-conscious about them, and failed. She was excited about a concert coming up in a week. Peter pledged to attend, with a guest. He didn't know who his guest would be.

Ed was very muscular, with heavy bones, thick wrists, broad short hands with a powerful grip. He had always been proud of his strength. Now he looked tired, abstracted, thoughtful, graying, thickening. But he wasn't old, only forty-two, forty-three. Peter couldn't remember which it was. It was easier to visualize Ed behind a barn splitting logs than in an office all day. Lil, vivacious by dinnertime, her voice unctuous, dark blond hair shining, painted eyes: blue, green, black, white. Her daily act of magical transformation again successful. Peter stared at them and wondered who they were. Ed, who had been his favorite person on earth once, who still was, he supposed, was strange to him. This unfamiliarity with what should have been familiar made him uneasy.

He was drawn again and again to Ed's lined face. Who was he? Why was he so old, so tired? What did he do, what did he know that cost him so heavily in years? The question brought only disquiet, a desire to be through with dinner, away from his brother.

"And what did you do at the office today, Daddy?"—"Oh, I wrote a couple of laws. It's illegal now to park your bike anywhere but in front of your own house, and you can't ride a boy's bike ever."—"Daddy! How could you!"—"For your own good, honey. For your own good."—"My brother is a senator from Pennsylvania. He has lunch with the President."—"Oh, really?"—"Sure, see the souvenir napkins? Here's one with coq au vin. And here's sloppy joe. And see that red stain? Burgundy."

"What?" Peter said. "Sorry, Lil. Woolgathering."

"I said, will you go with us to Wilmar Dukes' party Saturday? Mrs. Dukes specifically invited you today when I saw her."

"Oh, I don't ..."

"Parties at the Dukes house are always very nice," Lil said. "You never know who's going to be there. With what ax that needs grinding. One thing, nothing that's said there ever leaks to the press. I just don't know what he has over the press, but it's sacred ground."

"Do me a favor and come," Ed said. "In fact, if you'd escort one of the girls from the office, I'd appreciate it a lot. If you're up to it," he added quickly.

"Oh, I'm up to anything," Peter said. "But can't she just go?"

"Mrs. Dukes wouldn't invite an aide." Lil's laugh was not pleasant.

"I was going to wrangle her a date with someone, but

this would work out much better," Ed said. "She's a clever girl, D. C. MacMannus. She can pick up nuances, drift in and out of groups and spot the gist of the conversation in a flash. I would appreciate it."

Peter shrugged. "She's willing to go like that?"

"Yes. She'll use you for a few minutes, parade you before Mrs. Dukes once or twice, and then leave you alone. She won't push herself at you at all."

Peter laughed. "Can't wait to meet the clever D. C."

February night, too fast, dark before dark was due or wanted. Peter walked, thinking about darkness at night, light at day, darkness in daylight. Wondering when the headache would strike again. Wondering what he should do, wondering why he didn't want to do anything, go anywhere, knowing that he didn't want to die, that he wasn't living.

A neighbor's dog barked at him. Crazy black-tongued chow, claiming possession of the street, the air, the night. School seemed to belong to another life, not his, someone else's life where the goals had been set up early and kept in neat alignment ever after. And the goal that had been straight ahead was a chimera off to one side now, but nothing had replaced it. School was a word they mentioned now and then. It had no meaning to him at all. He wondered when Ed would stop being oblique about it, how he would respond.

"Peter, we have to have a talk. Now don't go all stiff-backed on me, or get apologetic, or anything. Man to man, boy. What are your plans?"—"Honorable, sir. Honorable. I think."—"You know what I mean. Are you going back for your doctorate? Why in Christ's name you didn't tell me when the reclassification came through I'll never know, but that's done with. Now there's the future to consider. You're young, you have a year or less to finish. You can go to Harvard, or to Columbia, back to Berkeley, whatever you want."—"I'm working over my thesis."—Ed, silenced. What can you say to someone who's writing a thesis?

Peter strode happily, feeling the cold on his face, swinging his hands to make a wind on them, to make them tingle, even hurt; feeling alive through his hands. The barking dog was silent now, but he would bark again when Peter returned. He wished Lil weren't so uptight about him.

Whispers, as clear as if spoken through speakers, through police microphones, megaphones. "Ed, I'm worried about him. He's so strange. Why doesn't he sleep?" They had been in Ed's study, he in the hall near the kitchen. Too far away to have been able to hear them.

"The wound. That happens sometimes, I've heard. He dozes, after all. They say that Edison, or was it Franklin, never really slept either. Catnaps."

"Is he all right mentally? You know."

"Of course he is."

Of course, he was, Peter echoed. The dog began to bark again.

Chapter 2

Ed finished tying his black shoes, flawlessly shined, expensive, and stared at them for a long time. He was tired, with a fatigue that long weekends of loafing didn't touch. Neither did skiing trips to Squaw Valley, or Colorado, or Switzerland. A small clock on the vanity table clicked softly as the minute hand passed the twelve, and he started. When he stood up, he took several deep breaths, squared his shoulders deliberately and left the bedroom, ready for another party, another long night.

Lil was at the far end of the hall, outside Peter's door. When she saw him approaching, she put her finger to her lips. He joined her at the door. The girls were in Peter's room.

"... If you're writing a book, how does it start?" Elaine asked.

"'Once upon a time,' of course, how else?"

"Books don't start like that any more."

"What books don't?"

"Any of them."

"Mine does. So what you really mean is that books that don't start like that, don't start like that. Books that do start like that, do start like that." Pause. "Isn't that what you mean?"

"Now it is."

In the hall outside the door Lil gave Ed a significant look.

"See what I mean?" she whispered.

"What do you mean?"

"He tells them terrible lies and makes them admit that they're true. It just isn't what I like to have someone do with them. It confuses them."

Ed sighed. "Let's go to the party." Louder, he called,

"Peter, ready?"

Ed drove to D. C.'s apartment and went in to fetch her. She came down wrapped from hooded head to toes in a dark cloak. "D. C., this is Peter. Miss MacMannus." He got behind the wheel and started the long drive to the Dukeses' house. Her hand was cool, her grip almost too hard for a girl, Peter decided. Lil talked about a book she was to review. No one seemed to be listening. At least no one contributed anything.

When Peter saw D. C. again, at the party, without the concealing outer cape, he saw that she was slender, and pretty, a standard good-looking American girl: healthy, wholesome, good skin, gleaming pale hair. Only her hands were not pretty. Big knuckles, crooked fingers, spatulate. He wondered if her knees were knobby, if her toes were ugly.

"There are zones," she said, steering him toward a room cleared for dancing. "This is old folks' corner. Foxtrots, minuets, the Charleston. Good place to talk. More seductions are begun here than almost anywhere else in Washington. Also it's the quickest way to the bars." A dozen couples were dancing, more people were clustered at the long tables that lined one wall.

"We might try a slow waltz toward the drinks," Peter said.

"Right. If there's anyone you should meet along the way, I'll introduce you." She smiled and nodded to people on the dance floor, waved to a woman framed in the doorway.

"Past Mrs. Dukes on the way?"

"Possibly. Why?"

"I'll throw myself at your feet in front of her, swearing to do violence to myself if you say no."

"Oh, that'll really go over big. She'd dog our footsteps throughout eternity waiting to see such a spectacle."

"Frankly, I think Mrs. Dukes is a frost."

"Isn't everyone? Nearly everyone."

"Who isn't?"

"Your brother. Senator Knute. A few more. Me, I hope. I'm not at all sure yet about you."

"I'm the frostiest of them all."

"Can you move just a little bit more? I can almost reach the champagne...."

He leaned past her and took a hollow-stemmed goblet from the breakfront, handed it to her.

"Thanks. Isn't there another one?"

"I'm a teetotaller."

"You're not!"

"What I am is a liar. What I want is a scotch, or possibly bourbon, or Irish. Anything but champagne. Decadent drink."

"Oh, damn. You should have said so. Hard liquor on the east side, wines and punch on the west side. Always. Shall we waltz back across the floor?"

"D. C., you look lovely tonight." Tall, pale man, hands like dangling doeskin gloves, waiting to be filled.

"Norman, this is Peter Roos. Norman Pryor." At the look of ignorance on Peter's face, she added gently, "The columnist, you know."

He didn't know, although probably he should. Stumbling into one of the blanks was always a surprise. He took the limp hand for a moment, and when he let it go, he was mildly interested that it didn't flop like a fish. He suffered the close scrutiny that Pryor gave him before turning his full attention to D. C. Pryor's eyes were penetrating, made a mockery of the other image he presented of ineffectual, effeminate, artistic hanger-on.

"D. C., you simply have to fill in some gaps for me, or the most distorted version of the hearings will be made public...."

Peter watched the party, hating it, wishing it were over, unable to withdraw because he was Ed's guest and it was important for him to be there. Important for D. C. to be there, he corrected. The first hour ended. Senator Dukes paused momentarily by Peter. Silver hair thin on top, long behind his ears, paunchy, hairy wrists, hairy fingers. Gracious. "Is there anything I can do for you, Peter? Anything at all?" Meaning it, apparently. He must have made a hidden signal to a waiter, who appeared silently with a tray. "Try one of these, Peter. Good honest sourmash whiskey. Only thing I touch." He took two of the glasses, handed one to Peter, then nodded to his wife, raised his glass to Peter and drifted away. Mrs. Dukes, corseted into a cylinder, shiny in a metallic dress, shellacked from head to silver-clad toes, ready to fire. She smiled at Peter, turned to say something to her husband. Peter saw D. C. again. Tall and slender, long, pale hair, held back sleekly by a ribbon that picked up the green of her dress that picked up the green of her eyes. Clever, clever D. C., parrying Pryor's questions adroitly, making him laugh. Peter admired the way she had learned to minimize her hands, how nearly invisible they were.

The party became louder, sedately noisy. Peter needed the drink Senator Dukes had given him. Too much noise made his head ache, made his hands perspire, and finally clench, and sometimes it brought on *the* headache.

The quietest place that Peter could find was in the seduction room, where couples still danced to fox-trot music that was provided live by five men who looked bored. He sat down as far from them as he could and tried not to hear the party. The columnist, Norman Pryor, ambled up to him and leaned against the wall.

"Bloody party, isn't it?"

"I've seen worse," Peter said.

"And better, I'll bet. You interested in politics?"

"No."

"Just as well. Addictive, you know. More kicks in politics than on a football field. How's your head?"

"Fine," Peter said. Pryor wasn't looking at him, but kept flicking his gaze out at the people on the dance floor, those at the bar, keeping a watch on the archway that led to the wide hall and the other rooms where a rock group was playing, and where people were readying tables for the buffet. Peter closed his eyes, willing the party to stop, the noise to stop. He could feel the throbbing of a vein in his temple. The room, overheated only moments before, seemed chilly now. "The only other game with any kick, I guess," he said, without opening his eyes, "is the science game. Instant rapport between scientists of all nations, everything from physics to parapsychology."

"You're a scientist, aren't you?" Pryor said softly. "I had forgotten that. You studied under Gregory Grange, didn't you?"

Peter opened his eyes suddenly and blinked, then lifted his glass and finished the drink quickly. He became aware that Pryor had gone very still, and glanced at him. Pryor was watching him thoughtfully.

When they had started working on his amnesia, they had sprung names at him randomly; with the electrodes on his scalp, the various machines measuring his blood pressure, his heart rate, his perspiration flow, they always knew instantly when they made a hit. And so painfully, slowly, over a period of ten months they had led him back to this self, this person called Peter Roos, with a background and past that were no longer areas of total blackness. He couldn't stop the sudden lurch in his stomach, and the involuntary tightening of muscles that the name Grange produced in him then. He hadn't thought of Grange in over three years. Pryor continued to regard him, and Peter finally managed a shrug.

"Is there an international science game?" Pryor asked softly.

"Not very damn likely, is it? I was just making polite party noises." He knew Pryor didn't believe him, and he didn't care. He closed his eyes again. In a moment he heard Pryor leave. Only then did he try to loosen his grasp on the glass he was holding.

A man and a woman danced near Peter and stopped several feet to his left. The woman was laughing. The throbbing in his temple increased. He got up carefully and left the room.

He heard his name called and turned to see Ed and Senator Knute coming toward him. He recognized Knute from television newscasts and newspaper photographs. He had been out of town for the past weeks, so they had not yet met, although he was Ed's closest friend in Washington. Ed made the introduction, then left them together.

Thomas Lynch Knute was very tall, six feet three, broad, with a large bony face, gray eyes, light hair that was thick and a little too long, not following fashion so much as out of carelessness.

"Call me Tom," he said, shaking Peter's hand with a steady pressure, "as soon as you feel that you can be comfortable with me. And until then don't call me anything. It's too hard to unlearn a name you stick on someone. Heading for the bar?"

"Yes, but slowly."

"So'm I. This way." Before he moved, he studied Peter openly, frankly, and suddenly smiled, and his smile was warm and personal and made him appear much younger than a senator should be. "Ed doesn't realize how much he's talked about you, I'm sure," he said then. "He's so damned anxious that we take to each other, I was prepared to boot you right off the planet on sight. I was beginning to feel like a homely girl being pushed out on a blind date, ready to despise the sucker. It would have been a mistake. Welcome home, Peter." Then he turned and led the way to the bar.

Peter got a bourbon on the rocks and Tom Knute a scotch and soda, and they moved away from the bar and stood near a wall, with the party before them, clusters of people talking, laughing, here and there a pair, or three people with heads close together in more serious conversations, D. C. with two men now, laughing at both of them, one of them the pale columnist, the other unknown; Ed and Senator Dukes and a four-star general talking... From the adjoining room the sound of acid rock, the clatter of silverware from yet another direction, laughter. It was a successful party.

"How long do these go on?" Peter asked.

"It's like a well oiled piece of machinery. Mrs. Dukes is a marvel at planning. Drinks from seven until ten, then a buffet from ten until eleven-thirty. The first guest departs at twelve, and by twelve-thirty all but a handful who have business to discuss have left. There might be eight or ten still here by one when black coffee is brought out." He finished his drink and reached past Peter to put the glass down on a table. "Mrs. Dukes will then say good-night and vanish and the business at hand is dragged out."

"Hard on the wives, isn't it?"

"They'll be sent home. You might be asked to escort Lil, and maybe my wife, home tonight, in fact."

"Not just a gratuitous invitation, then," Peter said.

"Nothing ever is around here."

Peter glanced at the tall senator, but his eyes were narrowed, and his gaze fastened on the huddle that was Ed, Wilmar Dukes and the general.

"Excuse me," Tom Knute said. "Think I'll drift over that way. See you again in a little while."

Because his head was aching, and he was drinking more than he usually did, and the fact that his dinner had been very early, therefore mostly uneaten, Peter was having trouble keeping the party in focus. And because a whole new set of memories had suddenly come to life, he added. The party had gone into slow motion, and the noise was like an electric circus now, pounding arrhythmically against his ears, catching him off guard with no defenses. He couldn't stop hearing snatches of conversations.

". . . million and a half worth of jewels . . ." Laughter, significant looks, more laughter.

". . . commission report . . ."

"I can get you an advance copy. . . ."

"I've got it. Tell you, quash the summary somehow. Goddamn non sequitur . . ."

". . . good kid, just needs a break. You know. Willing to do anything, anything at all . . ."

"So she went to Dr. Lockridge, in the city, Park Avenue, and all. And he said he hadn't delivered a baby on his couch in forty years of practice and wouldn't begin with her. The first abreaction probably would bring on labor. She's suing him for malpractice. Says it's his fault that she was in a state when she was admitted. . . ."

". . . not just splintered; shredded, cast to the wind is more like it. Going to take them ten, twelve years to put the pieces back together. . . ."

"Hey! Hungry?"

Peter felt a tug on his arm and turned to see D. C. at his side. She was carrying a champagne glass in which the bubbling drink no longer bubbled.

"Are these parties always this noisy?"

"Noisy? I must be used to these affairs. Now, if you'd asked if I think it's boring..."

Nearby a woman shrieked with laughter. She winced at the sound. "See what you mean." She nodded toward the far door that led to a room that he hadn't been in yet. "It's quieter over there; that is, if you're not eating."

"Had supper early with the children," he said. "Porridge and raisins with brown sugar and cream. In the upstairs nursery, with Nanny nearby."

She looked at him with a quick penetrating directness. "You're not easy," she said.

The crowd in the room had thinned, with people leaving for the buffet in the other direction. Through the open door D. C. led him into a smaller room that had a fireplace with a large log sputtering and hissing, burning with a feeble, orange flame and a lot of smoke. There were half a dozen other people in the room, talking quietly in two separate groups. D. C. went to the fireplace, where there was a large green leather chair. She sat on a cushion on the floor and motioned for him to take the chair. "Better?"

"Yeah." He looked past her at the damp log trying to burn. "I'm not really a crank," he said. "Unduly sensitive to noise is all."

"Oh." She looked at him, then asked, "Are you all right?"

"Sure. Did pasty face worm out of you the information he was after?"

"Past—... You mean Norman Pryor. Actually he didn't want anything. He had something to tell me."

"Is that the same drink you got when we arrived on the scene?"

She held it up and looked at the smeary glass. "I'm not much of a drinker. Especially at a party like this."

"Too busy gathering information?"

"Something like that." She looked up at him and

smiled. "Aren't you just a tiny bit too drunk to try to ride that white charger tonight?"

Peter laughed then and leaned back in the chair, closing his eyes. "Clever, clever Miss MacMannus. You win."

"But I'm not playing anything. Relax, Peter. Why don't you just relax a little?"

"Because I might fly apart and splatter all over everyone in the house."

"Okay, then hang on. But don't bait me, all right? I'm not out to get you."

"What are you out to get? Never mind. Delete that. Strike it out. Can I see you again?"

"Yes."

He looked down at her pale hair, with a nimbus lightened by the fire behind her making her appear almost haloed. "I'd like to talk to you, but not tonight because I expect to be called on for escort duty for some ladies. When can I see you?"

She had straightened slightly at his words, and now she touched her glass to her lips.

"You didn't know about the extracurricular meeting planned for tonight. Right? I managed to startle you after all."

"You continue to startle me, Peter. In many ways. But no, I didn't know about the meeting." She nodded to someone across the room, and he turned to see Norman Pryor framed by the doorway. D. C. turned again to Peter. "Will you walk out with me? I have to talk to either your brother or Senator Knute before they start that meeting, and I don't want it to appear that I am seeking out either of them."

Peter regarded her for a minute or more, then nodded. "I'm glad you're not out to get me," he said. "When do you not work?" He stood up and gave her his hand, helping her from the floor. "I'd like to see you when the most important thing on your mind is what you'll order for dessert."

She put her hand on his arm and they started to walk again, toward the dining room. "Why don't you give me a call?" she said. "I'm in the habit of eating dinner every night of the week." He noticed for the first time that she had a dimple in her left cheek.

"Peter, there you are." Tom Knute approached them, leading a small pregnant woman into the room. "Want you to meet Janice."

Peter had put Ton Knute in the same category as Ed: very likable, instantly attractive, do-gooder when doing good wasn't too difficult or costly, approaching middle age, settled. He found himself revising his opinion of Tom when he saw him with his wife. Now he seemed years younger than Ed, more vital and committed to living. Janice had the face of a child, a wise child that sees and understands and forgives all. She was near term, and he envied the child in her womb, envied her husband the bliss that must lie between her legs. She had the serenity of a madonna and the beauty. Especially between her and the canvas would the shadow always fall. He hoped that she would have many children; they would not age her and the world needed children borne of such a woman. That and more went on in the timeless interval of meeting her, holding her firm warm hand a moment, feeling exhilarated, awed even, by a presence that seemed extraordinary. The spoke to one another, her voice was low and throaty, and over it he could hear D. C. and Ed speaking.

"Grange is consulting with the President. He's going to testify at the DEDF hearings."

"Good God! Are you sure?"

"Certain."

"That's a good girl, D. C. Thanks."

"Peter will see you home, honey," Tom said. Janice nodded, smiling.

"I'll look you up at twelve or a little later," Janice said. She moved away at the side of her tall husband.

"I think I'm in love with her," Peter said wonderingly.

"Of course you are. Everyone is."

He looked at D. C. quickly, but her face was innocent of guile or spite. "She's thirty-two or -three, I forget which. He's thirty-nine. They have three children already. She has money, lumber, oil, land in Florida. Bryn Mawr."

"Enough already."

"I always get asked, if I'm around when someone first meets her."

"What's DEDF?"

"Deep Earth Defense Facilities. You do have good ears, don't you?"

"And Grange? Is that Gregory Grange?"

"I can see why you think it's a noisy party!"

"You don't want to tell me?"

"Don't be an idiot. There's no secret. Gregory Grange, out of Waverly Insitute, out of Harvard, out of Cal Tech. Presidential advisor on scientific matters. You know him?"

"Yeah. I studied under him."

D. C. was like an electronic engineer's dream of the most perfect receiver: sensitive to wavelengths that nothing else could perceive, sensitive to the most minute change in frequency, alert to all possible gradations of transmission. Something in Peter's voice that he didn't hear or order there alerted her. There was a slight increase in her tension, as if a current were flowing through a line that had been inert. There was no visible change, but he could sense a difference.

"You know," he said, "intrigues can be boring? Isn't there anyone at this party tonight who isn't working?"

"Never," she said. Then in one of her sudden changeabouts she said, "Peter, watch out for Pryor. He's asking questions about you. I don't know why, but he can be bad news."

He shrugged and when she left him, he returned to the green leather chair by the sputtering fire and waited for twelve o'clock. He would gather his ladies about him and tie them all together with a silken string and open his wings. With one gigantic flap he would fly into the black sky, towing them behind him, and one by one drop them into their own nests. And he would go to his room, where it would be dark, and pleasantly warm, and very quiet. And then, he thought, then he would take his finger out of the dike, and let the memories in.

Chapter 3

Ed's house was a fine, large, old-fashioned building, with high-ceilinged rooms that had as many windows as outside wall space permitted. Someone had understood about windows and instead of covering them with layers of curtains and drapes like an ante-bellum maid's layers of petticoats, had treated the yard like a large screen, with staggered plantings that let the air and light flow, but allowed privacy inside the house. Outside Peter's windows there was the big oak tree, and beyond it, between the house and the street and the houses across the street, a row of sweeping spruces. His room was comfortable, and although he had been there only two weeks, he had come to feel that it was a special refuge. There was an easy chair and lamp for reading, a mahogany four-poster bed, a desk with a good light, stationery and pens, and a portable typewriter, two bureaus, one with a tall mirror above it topped by an angry eagle whose head brushed the ceiling. The floors throughout the house were parquetry, and with unsuspected wisdom, or through economy, Lillian had not covered them, except with throw rugs, and some good Kirmans downstairs. On Peter's floor there were three shaggy brown rugs, so that when he paced, as he did almost every night, he reminded himself of a mountain goat with one foot on lush grass and the other on a rocky streambed. He paced with his shoes off—even his slippers sounded loud on the wood floors.

There had been something that one of the doctors had said, Dr. Seligman. "I didn't think we'd ever get this much back, Peter. I don't think there are any more big holes, but from time to time you'll find that you're filling in the details. Names, faces. Details."

Details! he thought. Grange a detail!

And Lucy a detail? He stopped pacing, one foot higher than the other, and closed his eyes hard. Three goddamn years! Three fucking goddamn years!

He started to walk again. Pacing, thinking-not-thinking. Not word thinking. A visual, emotive imagery and feeling experience that brought scenes to focus, swirled them away to be replaced by other hurtful scenes. Lucy under the redwoods. Lucy in his bed, in his arms. The lab. Walking on a gravel path between university buildings. Glimpses of that other life that was suddenly alive in his memory, even though it seemed to be someone else's past, not his. He could look at it, see himself in the scenes, at one and the same time living it, and feeling a distance that was immeasurable. "Dissociation," the doctor had said. "It happens with amnesiac patients sometimes."

He sat at the window and stared out at the darkness. And a scene played in his head.

Grange, strapped from hips to shoulders because of an accident that had wrenched his back, sitting upright in a wheelchair while six graduate students lounged on the grass at his feet. His backyard with the grill that he had made, the benches he had made, the picnic table that he had made, steaks that he grilled as he waved away smoke that curled about his face. He was the Delphic oracle, wreathed in holy smoke, speaking riddles of infinite wisdom.

"The truly creative, intelligent young people are turning more and more to science. They are attracted by the same mysteries that lure the artist and the painter and the poet. But they aren't content to remain on the outside mucking about with metaphysical nonsense." He arranged the steaks on the grill, grease sputtered, flared with more smoke that seemed to seek him out, him alone. "Lucy, my dear, will you wheel the salad cart this way. Ah yes, garlic... Here it is." The garlic was neatly minced, ready to use; he sprinkled it over the steaks. The steaks were a ritual; it was his body that he was serving, and the wine that stood "breathing" was his blood.

"If an artist stumbles across a maze, he will rejoice in the new mystery, and he will paint it, adding to its mysteries those dredged from his own shitty dreams. The poet will moan about the beauty or awesome aspects of it." His voice dripped sarcasm. He turned the steaks, waved smoke vigorously, sipped wine. Only he was allowed wine before food was served. "But the scientist, no less awed and mystified, no less overwhelmed by beauty and the unknown, will examine it. His viewpoint will include all the sensibilities of the artist and poet, and still there is more. He is a puzzle solver. He alone of the truly gifted, creative people must solve puzzles, not merely report them. True creativity is demonstrated in the questions a real scientist asks."

Grange was looking at his watch, apparently ignoring the steaks. Suddenly he moved, sweeping a platter from the salad cart, spearing the nearest steak at the same instant. Dinner was ready. Now everyone had wine. He proposed the toast.

"To you, the inheritors."

Stein said, "The thing about art is how it lasts, great art, I mean. And scientific discoveries are being superseded all the time."

"Art that is truly great is no longer being created, my boy. Look about you today. The artists among us are scientists. No one is creating great, enduring works of fiction, or poetry. Those few who display some evidence of potential greatness are overwhelmed by chaos which in their hands becomes ever more chaotic. Art is the transformation of chaos into order. What our would-be artists are giving us is chaos distorted by schizophrenic tendencies. We have no art. No literature. Today's music is nothing more than an assault on our auditory nerves."

Lucy stirred restlessly. She was a violinist, and talked occasionally of giving up her graduate work to become a serious musician. Grange fastened his gaze on her. He was always harsher on Lucy than on any of the rest of them. She was probably the most gifted of them all.

"Wherever the scientist turns his attention, there is an infinite regression of beauty that the ignorant artist, whatever his field is, can never suspect, much less appreciate. Creativity without mastery of the subject matter is childish finger painting with shit."

"But art as neat and orderly processes wasn't enough," Lucy said softly. "There is more than the mechanical man of the nineteenth century. More than the biochemical processes. There is also man of the transcendental experience. Man of the chaos that you mentioned. It's part of him too. Man as mystery. Intuitive, sometimes precognitive, sometimes clairvoyant. You can't express these qualities in neat and orderly schemata. There is a chaos of the soul that man right now is examining, for perhaps the first time."

"Good Christ, now we'll talk about the soul!" His eyes narrowed and a look of near malevolence came and went swiftly. Grange's face was almost bland, very smooth, no deep lines, and although he wore glasses on occasion, he was not wearing them that day. He was very vain, always impeccably dressed, his small narrow hands manicured flawlessly; he kept abreast of fashion without effort. Once when a careless student had left acid on a bench and it had ruined Grange's trousers he had made the class reimburse him. Someone had questioned the amount—eighty-five dollars—and he had produced a receipt from his tailor. Now when he spoke to Lucy, his voice was thick with sarcasm.

"With the proper conditioning today I can produce any affective state of the soul that you, or anyone else, orders." Lucy started to speak and he silenced her with a wave of his hand. "You think the personal revelations aren't conditioned? Don't be an ass. He's the most determined operator of all, the poor transformed slob who can't bear life without myth and gods."

Lucy shook her head. "I think the real retreat from reality is in the assumption that man is a windup toy. The existential man is not a whole man."

"That's good," Grange said. "Very good. Look at it this way. There are souls, created by brains developed enough to educate themselves. How many of your mankind out there have that ability? One in a thousand? One in five thousand? If he can't do it for himself, someone else has to wind him up. Or eliminate him. Eat, eliminate, procreate. There's your man with a chaotic soul. Existence without meaning. Why shouldn't someone with a soul wind him up each morning, give him something to do, derive some good from him?"

"Because the reality of life isn't known yet, not by you, not by anyone who would do the winding up. And with every push forward that we make in any of the fields exploring it, that reality recedes. You talked about the infinite regression of beauty. I know. The submicroscopic world is incredibly lovely, but its reality also recedes. Until it reaches the subatomic level, where there is again chaos instead of order."

Grange laughed abruptly. "You're a Goddamn Jesuit, my dear. I should know better than argue with a woman. You want your mysteries, have them. Be my guest. But, Miss Boardman, I predict. No, more than that. I state categorically that within ten years we will have at our disposal the knowledge, and the hardware, to produce whatever kind of man we decide is best fitted for this world. In whatever quantities we want."

Lucy stared at him a moment, then lowered her gaze to her hands in her lap. "Like cattle, so many head at a time."

"Exactly," Grange said, strangely smug and amused.

That was Grange. That was the year following his Nobel prize for the RNA work. The second in his career. The first one had been when he was only twenty-three, and that too was for work in genetics. Now he was special advisor to presidents. Seeing him again in that timelessness that was memory, Peter could hear the tone of his voice, the inflections, the mockery. Then he had heard only the words and had swum in a sea of ideas that seemed to support his most ambitious dreams. But then he had known who he was, why he was there, where he was going. He had been one of the new inheritors, and the glances he had flicked out over the world were scornful and possessive. And hungry. He had wanted his inheritance.

His lamp was turned off. In the black yards were islands of light, from the hall, the front porch, the dressing

room of the master suite. A car turned into the driveway
and quietly entered the garage, a door opened, closed, Ed
was home. Peter sat down and waited for him to go to his
room. He didn't want to talk to him, to hear his troubles,
or be implored to share his own. He had no troubles to
share. He shouldn't have brought back the scene with
Grange. Thinking about Grange meant thinking about
Lucy.

He listened to Ed's slow ascent, his slow progression
down the hallway. His steps were too heavy for a man as
young as he was. Quiet returned, and the islands of light
drowned, plunging the entire yard into dark. It was
almost three. Perhaps he would sleep. Sometimes he did.
But not yet. The world was becoming solid, a great
nothingness was absorbing everything into itself. He sat
at the window and watched the blackness overtake the
trees, the shrubs, everything. The sky was very dark with
heavy clouds. It would snow. The smell of approaching
snow was in the air. At four-fifteen it started, and he knew
he wouldn't sleep.

He drifted to earth on snowflakes, rose as fast as
thought to the highest of the clouds and drifted down
again, swirling gently, soundlessly, bringing incredible
beauty to the city. He wondered if it was snowing where
Lucy was, and deliberately turned his thoughts from her,
to anyone else. To Grange. Would Grange awaken and
find it lovely? Or would it interfere with his plans for the
day, make transportation difficult? He wondered if
Grange was the one who had betrayed him.

Chapter 4

On Sunday morning Peter overheard Bobby and Elaine in a discussion. Elaine was practicing her flute part for the concert.

"I mean, what good is it? You play a few songs and things, people clap and go home. For what?"

"It's pretty, that's for what."

"Well, I wouldn't practice for hours and hours. I'd rather make Barbie clothes, or build a snowman. You want to go out now?"

"I can't. I have another half hour to practice." A few sweet trills, then she stopped and said, "When I grow up I'll travel all over the world and play my flute, and Johnny will play the violin."

Bobby made a rude sound. "If I grow up I'm going to live by the ocean and swim and fish every day, with Peter."

Peter shivered at her words. So matter of fact. Accepting the "if" qualification without question.

Bobby and Peter played in the snow for hours that afternoon, making snow sculptures of geese, of bears, a funny crooked man with a crooked stick. Elaine joined them and they used up all the snow in the large yard, and when they returned to the house they left behind a fairyland of white figures that were already turning gray, that were blackening fast on the level surfaces where soot lodged.

Later, Ed dozed by the fire while Peter leafed through the paper, tired from the snow play, aware of a dull headache that persisted. Lil was napping before dinner and the girls had lessons to do. The large house was very quiet. Peter wasn't reading anything; an occasional ad caught his eye, an artist's conception of a subdivision of

the future, a headline about pollution, another about the
latest in arms control. He didn't read the brief article
about the hearings, or if he did, he wasn't aware of it until
he realized that Ed had said something to him.

"Eliot Noble is so tame that he doesn't even need a
collar and tag," Peter said.

Ed sat upright and blinked. "What? What did you
say?"

"Didn't you ask me what I thought about Eliot?"

Ed stared at him, then slowly shook his head. "Hell,
maybe I did. I was wondering what you thought of him
now."

Then Peter remembered the article. "You and Eliot are
both on that subcommittee, aren't you? The one holding
hearings on the underground defense projects? DEDF."

"You saw the article then?"

"I must have," Peter said. "Eliot's coming to dinner
tonight?"

"Yes. He wants to make certain that I understand the
President's positon," Ed said drily.

Peter turned another page. He didn't want to talk
about politics, or underground facilities, or Eliot Noble,
whom they both had known all their lives. He turned
another page, and there was the article. He hadn't read it
yet.

Slowly he read the brief story, only two paragraphs
long. The Subcommittee on National Policy, chaired by
Senator Wilmar Dukes, would conduct hearings in
March to consider the Joint S-H bill proposed by Senator
Carl Marko, R., California, to initiate a study of the
feasibility of placing all defense facilities deep underground to protect them against any future attack.

Ed was staring broodingly at the fire, and Peter
continued to hold the newspaper before him, no longer
seeing it, feeling a chill that had nothing to do with
weather, or the news.

Ed must have been muttering under his breath, he
decided. And he knew that his hearing had been affected
curiously by the head injury. In the hospital they had
tested him with elaborate equipment, and in the end had

simply accepted what seemed an impossibility. He could hear sound levels and frequencies that should not have been audible to the human ear. No explanation. Ed must have been muttering under his breath, he repeated to himself. And he had always been attuned to Ed. Always.

Ed was sixteen years older than Peter, with three sisters between them. He had taught Peter to swim, how to use a bow and arrow, how to skate, ride, ski. Everything. Peter had mourned for him when he left for school, and when he was drafted during the Korean War, Peter had made a deal with God. He could see himself again, in the Pennsylvania bedroom, kneeling at the open window with twenty-below-zero weather freezing him. "God, I promise, if they hurt Ed, I'll go over there and kill them all myself." He was six then. Later he bargained with God. "If you don't let him die, I'll sing in the choir." He did, for over a year.

Ed was the living legend that breathed life into the books that Peter read: King Arthur became real because of Ed. Ahab took on meaning. Deerslayer lived through him. Without him Peter never would have known what a hero was. There was none of the responsibility of the father-son relationship, none of the hostility, none of the guilt; nothing but the love that Peter forced on him, even though, in the beginning especially, it was not wanted.

When the doctor gave Peter a choice of hospitals where he could be an outpatient, without hesitation he had chosen Walter Reed, not because of the excellent facilities or the qualifications of the doctors there, but because, like a puppy that had been hurt beyond endurance, he wanted to creep back to the one person whom he had loved without doubt, who had never betrayed that love.

During that timeless period, the months he was fed with needles and tubes, drained with more tubes, cleansed by unfelt hands, kept alive when the flesh would have died, alterations had taken place in his brain. And when he had awakened, he was a new person: no past, no history, no name, nothing. They had taught him how to walk, how to talk, how to exercise his left hand and leg so that the paralysis was defeated finally. But they hadn't been able to teach him to love again. He was no longer blinded by the flashing, brilliant love that he had felt for Ed; he could see past the aura to the man behind the light now. Like the goal that had sustained him through years of school, the part-time jobs, the unspeakable food, the sleepless nights when sleep still had been a blessing, the goal that had dissolved to nothing and left a hole, so also that absolute love that was gone had left a vacuum that he scrabbled to fill and didn't know how. He had come home to Ed in terror because he sensed the void when he turned his gaze inward, and instead of the reassurance he had expected, he had found that there was another void. Snake eyes, he thought. Fathomless, endless chutes to hell. What had been the given, the bedrock, had been taken away.

Peter had dreamed once of a room where the pictures hadn't touched the surface of the wall behind them. They had been very important in the dream, important and isolated. That was how his memories of the past had become. Bits here and there. Isolated from other bits. Then in July most of the bits had flowed back together and he knew who he was again. And the headaches had started.

"They removed fragments of the missile within four hours of the injury, and they operated again ten days later to take out some more," the doctor had said, explaining slowly, watching Peter closely, as if this were not the first time he had gone through the same routine with him. "You lost a bit of brain tissue, too, you know."

When they probed and scraped, had they pried loose a section labeled "love" and raked it out with the junk and flushed it down the toilet?

Dinner at Ed's house when there were guests was an ordeal Peter had learned to cope with very early. He smiled pleasantly, said little, and never lingered over coffee. That night he excused himself as soon as he could, knowing that Ed would murmur something about his injury, the need for rest, and that the others would nod with understanding, and nurse their unasked questions.

He sat at the window and looked at the ghostly figures that rose from the ground, alien, contorted figures that would march and dance as soon as the house lights were turned off. The crooked man would chase the bears, threatening them with his crooked stick, stumble over the stupid geese, whose necks were too short, because with longer necks the heads kept falling off, so chop, another four inches of neck gone, replace the head and watch it fall off. Chop. They were short-necked geese.

He wondered if Ed knew that his daughter wasn't entirely certain that she would live to grow up.

At fifteen before twelve he knew he was getting one of the headaches. It started as a throbbing behind his eyes, a pressure deep in his skull, a volcano so deep that nothing could reach it. He took one of the capsules the doctor had given him. Synthetic morphine? Plastic medicine? He lay on the bed with his eyes closed. The throbbing increased, and now he could feel his eyeballs expand and contract with it. The medicine didn't help. They pretended they knew what caused the headaches, and what would alleviate them. They had reassured him, promised him that the headaches would go away. Maybe they had believed that. He only knew that synthetic morphine didn't help. Now with each outward thrust of the regular throbbing, there was a burning pain, a flashing searing pain that started deep and went out in all directions, hurting his eyes especially, tightening the muscles at the back of his neck, clenching his hands. With the worsening of pain his left side began to spasm and at the peak, the paralysis returned, as if the rehabilitation therapy had been only superficial. He thought how good it would be to go out into the snow, bury his head in the snow, let it fill his mouth, his ears, his nostrils. He knew that he couldn't call out. He kept that in mind, that he could not call for help. No one could help him.

The throbbing grew, increased in tempo, built up faster and faster to a searing pain, reached a crescendo of pain and held there. The pressure of the bed against his head was too much; he had to move. Deep inside him was the will to run. Run away from it. Run! He thought of the snow, not with words now, but an image, a blanketing, soothing, relieving whiteness that would cover him and protect him for all time. He tried to move, but the paralyzing pain made him forget how. He couldn't call out ... couldn't ...

Run! Run! It was more insistent, the need to run away from the pain. He tried to move again, rolled, fell to the floor, catching the nightstand on his way down. The stand fell across his shoulders.

There was knocking on his door. Ed entered, with Lil close behind him.

"My God! Peter!"

"Ed, what is wrong with him? What's wrong?"

Ed's voice was saying again and again, "My God!" Thick with unwanted understanding, horror. "Go to bed, Lil. You can't do anything here. I'll stay with him. Go to bed."

Peter realized that they had him on the bed again. He had no memory of having been lifted. He didn't open his eyes. Then he heard Ed weeping for him; Ed didn't know he was aware. Aware, with his head exploding in pain again and again and again. He expanded and filled the room with pain, then collapsed to a white hot point. Expanded, collapsed. He would lose consciousness, he knew, and willed it to happen. Willed death to happen. Then he would sleep.

Chapter 5

Peter moved and a tingling in his arm and leg, up and down his whole side, awakened him. Again, he thought. He moved cautiously, balancing himself on the bed until he was certain he could stand, then keeping his right hand on the bed frame, on the chair, the wall, he staggered to the bathroom. The tingling in his bad side became pins and needles that were mildly painful. He relieved himself, and drank a glassful of water, then another. He didn't know how long it had been this time, long enough to distend his bladder and to dehydrate him somewhat. He returned to bed, walking more steadily. He would doze now, he knew. Doze and awaken, doze again, until gradually the periods of wakefulness touched, and then he would be ready to get up.

Ed tiptoed in, stood over him a moment, looking at him. Peter pretended to be sleeping still. He didn't want to talk to Ed yet. He didn't think he could talk to anyone just yet. It was nearly dawn, the false darkness that pretended that morning was yet hours away, when all the while it was gathering strength to make the climb over the horizon. Peter willed the white creatures back to their places, willed the oak tree to concentrate on its renewal, reminded the spruces that were ideas only in the formlessness of predawn, of how they must spread and sweep and touch the ground to make hidey-holes for Bobby and the squirrels. Later, he listened to Lil and Ed talking in the hall, in their bedroom.

"I don't care if he is your only brother. I'm the one who was here with him all day. What if he'd had another attack? He needs hospital care. Anyone could see it."

"I'm sure if the doctors thought so they would have said so."

"And what about that man in the Texas tower? The doctors didn't put him in a hospital either, did they?"

"He isn't like that, and you know it. He told us that he got violent headaches from time to time. We just underestimated what he meant by violent, that's all."

"He had a fit! What if he did it again in front of the girls? Or at the Dukes party?"

"Honey, I told you I have an appointment to see his doctor."

"Ed, was he ever like that . . . before?"

"No. Of course not."

Peter drifted, not asleep, not yet really awake, and in that state he visualized his brother and Lil. Ed would be stretched out, his hands under his head, the way he had slept when still a boy. Lil would be taut, afraid, her world suddenly threatened by something unknown, unpredictable.

Peter shivered and drew the blanket up tighter about his neck, but the chill seemed to be coming from within, not from the room, and there was no way he could get warm.

He was getting glimpses of scenes; they flashed across his visual field quickly, grew to life size in full color, then vanished, to be replaced by other scenes.

Office work for an hour, answering letters, reading over D. C.'s wrap-up of the day's hearings. Back and forth between hearings and the Floor from ten until one. Warm, polished, gleaming wood panel wainscoting in a hallway. Lunch. Hearings from two until five or later. Long tables cluttered with ashtrays, water glasses, carafes of ice water. Meeting with Knute, Noble, a couple from Pennsylvania, others. Home and dinner. No time. No time. Have to forego the Commerce Subcommittee hearings, as well as the Judiciary full committee hearings. Read a synopsis. Call Ford again. Bastard. Peter rolled over, rubbed his eyes to dispel the visions. They weren't even his visions, he thought aggrievedly.

Peter felt himself slipping into a dream world. He should protest, he thought. He wasn't even asleep. The landscape was surreal, a door in the middle of nowhere. In the dream Ed was approaching the door. Now a man was painting a sign on the door. It said: Fission Department. Ed had a slip of yellow paper that he handed the man. Five. That was a high priority number. The headman studied him, wondering if there was enough gray matter to split five ways, then shrugged. He only worked here. He positioned Ed and turned on the amber lights, watched the smoke roll from flasks, saw the lightning arc between quivering silver steeples, watched the dials and meters race erratically. The hum became a Ta-dum-da-dum, da, dum, dadum, dadum-dadum. . . . Too much. Five was too high for him. The safety dial was edging into red when he got an inspiration. He reset the controls, and this time the gray matter was to be sliced four ways. The one to take care of Lil didn't need anything above the waist. When it was over, the five Eds walked out, each heading in a different direction, taking no notice of the others, each intent on the one small area that was his to service. Success. Lil never noticed that hers was whole from the waist down only.

Lil's voice scrambled the dream. "I never saw you cry before, not even when Elaine was being born and I was screaming in pain." She was jealous of Peter's agony. Ed sighed, and tossed restlessly.

At the other end of the hall, through two closed doors, with one ear pressed down hard on his pillow Peter stared into darkness, chilled. He couldn't have heard her whisper. Hallucinations, then. Audio hallucinations? Gradually the warmth of the blanket overcame his shivering and he closed his eyes and dozed.

Chapter 6

"How long will the hearings last?" Peter asked. The girls were in bed, Lil seeing to something of importance upstairs, and for once no company. Peter ached, there were sore spots on his shoulders, his neck was stiff. But, even more, he was tense with memories of pain and apprehension, and with the knowledge that this attack had been different.

Ed was nervous, restless. He didn't look directly at Peter. "Couple of weeks probably. We keep having new names added to the list of witnesses. Why?"

"Thought I'd like to come see, if they're public."

"Sure. Daily from ten until twelve-thirty, two until five or five-thirty. How are you feeling?"

And the something of importance that Lil had to see about came out into the open. She was outside the door; Peter could hear her breathing.

"Okay. Sorry to have alarmed you and Lil, though."

"I talked to Dr. Krump today. . . ."

"Isn't that a great name: Jeremiah Frederick Krump . . ."

"And he says that in the beginning the headaches, while less violent perhaps, were almost continuous, but the intervals are growing farther and farther apart now and he foresees a complete cure in a year or two."

Peter watched him silently, waiting, posing the unanswerable question: is it better to have a little evil all the time, or the maximum evil occasionally? Ed's skin was an unhealthy gray, pouches under his eyes the color of puffballs, and, like puffballs, they looked as if they would burst if touched. Is this what government did to men, Peter wondered, thinking of the "before" and "after" photographs that the newspapers liked to print of Presidents. Healthy, vital men entering the White House, to emerge from the other side used up, ancient, cynical or beaten down. Chronos and his children.

Ed paused. Beside him on an end table was his briefcase, not opened yet, but ready to gush forth papers and reports and memos. His hand strayed to it now and then, to pat it absently, like a pregnant woman feeling her belly.

"So, did he tell you anything that I didn't tell you?" Peter asked as the pause lengthened.

"No," Ed said, much too quickly, with too much emphasis. "No. But after seeing you, the intensity of the pain, and how it left you today. I mean, a picture worth a thousand books, sort of thing, you know. Anyway. Will you join my staff for the next year or two? Until you're ready to go back to school, if that's what you decide to do."

"Nepotism?"

"Not even my worst enemy can ever accuse me of that. Goddamn! I need someone with some science background on my staff. I've tried to get someone and failed. You'd be useful to me." He rummaged in the briefcase then and tossed Peter a list of books and articles. "I'm supposed to read all that for background material for the DEDF hearings. Three people on the staff have made a start at them, and they've all handed in reports so confused and garbled that I can't make heads or tails out of them. . . ." He looked toward Peter, then averted his eyes and looked again at the briefcase. "Peter, I need you. Just for the next few months, say you'll stay and let me put you on the payroll. You'll earn it."

Ed wouldn't lie to him, Peter thought suddenly and felt guilty over having such a thought. But Ed was lying, or had lied. And he didn't know about what. He held the list without looking at it. A few years ago if Ed had said, drop that and come help me, he would have dropped the world to run to him. And Ed needed help. He said slowly, "I just don't know right now. Let me think about it for a few days. I thought I might go up to Harvard after my next examination."

Hope or relief livened Ed's face briefly.

"Sure, sure. Let me know. And now I have to get at some of this stuff." He fished his glasses from his breast pocket and holding them, ready to put them on, he asked, "When you're awake night after night, what do you do?"

"Not much. Think, read, meditate. Walk now and then. Write a little. Taught myself to read music. Study, try to keep up with the journals again. I lost out on them for three years or more. A lot happened in that time."

Ed nodded. "You'd be like a second brain for me," he said, and suddenly his face flushed.

Peter looked at him questioningly. Ed laughed, but unease made the sound strange. "Nothing," he said. "A crazy dream I had. Wouldn't it be great if we could all divide ourselves from time to time, then regroup at will?"

Divisible brain, Peter thought, and the dream was fresh in his memory. But whose memory was it? Whose dream had it been? He started to rise; Ed waved him down again.

"Can't you read in here for awhile?"

"Sure. He picked up the evening paper and leafed through it, paying little attention to the items until he found himself scanning the want ads, apartments for rent. Lil coughed outside the door and he hastily closed the paper. She came in carrying a tray with a silver coffeepot and cups.

"Is it going to be one of those nights?" she asked Ed.

"'Fraid so." He indicated the stack of reading material.

"Anything I can do?"

He smiled at her, shaking his head. Peter tried not to see the exchange, tried not to give the impression of being intrusive. He thought about turning to the want ads, apartments for rent. He hadn't consciously decided to move, but it was an attractive idea. Whatever he had sought in coming to Ed's house, he hadn't been able to find it. And suddenly he knew he didn't want to live so close to his brother. Lil cleared her throat. He looked at her.

"Peter, can I ask you something rather personal? If you'd rather not talk about it, I'll understand. I mean, just say so."

Ed looked up too now, his face set and hard, regarding her almost as if she were a ragged stranger extending a bit of candy to his child.

"Go ahead, Lil," Peter said.

"When you get those headaches. I mean, is there a warning? It doesn't just hit hard, does it?"

"No. It takes a couple of hours to reach the peak. There's always time to get out of where I am, get to my room, take my pills and lie down."

She blushed, and was not pretty. Her nose darkened, the effects of the reddening under a sallow-toned makeup. She averted her gaze, not looking at either of the men. "I'm sorry, Peter. I didn't know how else to ask, except to just ask."

"Forget it, Lil. I should have explained them better when I got here. I . . . I guess I hoped it wouldn't come up."

She remembered the coffee and attacked it with relief. She used domesticity like a shield.

Peter took the offered cup, added cream, refused sugar. He pretended to read a sports item. But he was wondering about Lil; did her nose turn dark like that with passion? Did she have passion? Did Ed?

"Aren't you having coffee, too?" Ed asked her.

"No. I'm afraid it will keep me awa . . . I think I'll go up now, leave you to your work." She stood up and looked uncertainly at Peter. "There's a whole pot of coffee. The hot plate under the sunburst will keep it. If you'll just pull the plug when you are finished . . ."

"Sure, Lil. Good-night."

She crossed the room to kiss Ed on the cheek. He barely looked up from the journal he was reading. "Night, dear," he said, and returned to the article.

Peter got to the end of the feature on basketball and realized that he didn't know a thing he had read. He went to the top of the column of print to start over.

Ed was not reading when Lil left the room. He listened to her footsteps and felt a cold anger within him. What Peter represented to her, he thought, was something raw and wild, unknowable and frightening. And she was one of those cool women who had forsworn anything wild and raw at puberty. She never even undressed until the light was turned out. She couldn't face the reality of the flesh. Sweat, blood, pain disgusted her, or, he wondered, excited her? He had read somewhere that people like Lil were constantly repressing all the animalism in themselves, that the fight never let up. He shook his head and rubbed his eyes. It was too late for them, too late to try to understand the woman he had married, too late to give a damn if he ever understood her. And he knew that she would never forgive Peter his headache that she had witnessed, because it spoke of hidden things, of things never aired, of souls and hearts and bowels of man that one pretended out of existence. For Lil distancing was as automatic as breathing, as necessary as eating.

It hadn't been a good marriage for Lil, he thought suddenly. Passionately devoted to books, her library work in the Meet the Authors Society, a very good critic, she should have gone into it in some way that would have allowed her to gain recognition of her abilities. An avid first-nighter, she wrote perceptive reviews that occasionally appeared in the *Post*, or in a small magazine. Her book reviews were sharp and to the point, and she had a literary memory that helped her spot allusions and influences. She should have married a university professor in the arts, an English literature teacher, perhaps, or a scholar in the Elizabethan theatre. She should have become one herself. She would have blossomed then.

He wondered how she acted, what she said to those authors whom she met at the library teas. She would come home with her cheeks flushed, her eyes alive and happy, only to lapse back into the mundane world of children and home, or an obvious topic such as a popular movie, or television program, when his friends were there.

Once, when Bobby was an infant, he had tried to talk to her about their marriage, and he had seen the fear in her eyes. She had reviewed a sex manual in scalding terms, blistering the authors, and the readers, the publishers for letting it see print, the bookstores for handling it. Ed hadn't read the book, but he said that her review made him want to very much. She had torn the review into shreds and thrown them into the wastebasket.

"Everyone isn't like that," she had said. "Thank God! Ed, are you unhappy with me?"

"No, you know I'm not."

"Then let's just leave it all alone."

But she hadn't asked if he was happy with her. She hadn't said that she was happy with him. What she had said, not in words, but in her expression and her fears that showed that night, was that she refused to examine herself, that it was too humiliating to make the kind of self-examination that might lead to eventual change. And they had settled down again into a union without passion that was not uncomfortable, but was never ecstatic. They walked hand in hand, and would never fly, Ed thought, and shook himself almost violently.

She never had asked about other women, never hinted that she suspected there was someone else from time to time. None of the other women had ever led to anything serious, and Ed didn't know if he should be regretful or glad about that.

Peter continued to sit with the newspaper raised, his hands too tight and hard on it now. Sudden, unexpected sexual need was like a maelstrom whose outer edges included his head and his feet, his hands. He counted to ten, without moving, then counted more slowly, and the intensity passed, and if there was pain, it was of a different sort, the pain of absence, of nonfulfillment. Deep inside him something said over and over: Lucy. Lucy. He wondered how a man like Ed learned to live with a woman like Lil. Did he let her convince him that her way was proper? Did he have a girl somewhere who oiled and scented her body, and had mirrors, and lamps with red shades, and animal skins on the floor? He realized Ed was speaking to him.

"Are you all right?" Ed's voice was weary. "I mean, would you be willing to read through this for me? I can't make those little fishhooks come up with any meaning tonight."

Peter took the magazine, *The Journal of the Atomic*

Scientists, turned to an article by Marvin Poole. "I'm beginning to feel like Old Home Week," he said. "First Grange, now Poole."

"You know them both?"

"Sure. You can't be in graduate school in Berkeley without meeting the drawing names sooner or later, if only to bow at their feet."

"They both are to testify for the National Science Advisory Board. Taking opposing sides, naturally. A majority report and a minority report. Pays your money and takes your choice."

Peter glanced at the article: A *Study of the Effects of Subterranean Atomic Explosions on Rock Strata, Water Tables, and Other Geologic Formations.* "Why do you need this?"

"When witnesses request an appearance they often submit papers or other materials that they think will fill in some of the background of the material that they intend to cover. It never helps. We still have to go over it inch by inch, syllable by syllable, but I try to grasp the feel of the testimony with a little more information than I have already. What do you think of Poole?"

Peter closed his eyes and thought. He said finally, "Probably ten or twelve generations of gentlemen have bred him, and it shows. If we had kings, he'd be in line for succession. Four generations of Green Mountain Boys there, too. Thin, wiry, hard, and tough. Incorruptible, absolutely without question honest, and demands it from others. If he has friends, they must be as tough and hard and honest as he is. Or they couldn't stand him. Walked to school every day all weather with only a sweater, a thick sweater, but no more than that. And it gets cold in Massachusetts. Forgive you your first mistake with patience, forgive the second one, without patience, shoot you for the third."

Ed nodded, "Not a witness to win friends and influence people, I take it. Why is it always the Pooles who oppose men like Grange?" He shook his head. "There is a mystery about what kind of man succeeds as a scientist," he said. "Take Grange and Poole, two opposites in every way. But they share science. There has to be something that binds them together, something I haven't been able to find. I've looked for it in you, thinking that by having you at hand maybe I could puzzle it out, but if you've got it, I can't find it. I suspect you do."

"What is the common denominator among senators? Or window washers?"

"Let's stick to what I know," he said. "Senators. Ambition for power, for prestige, the urge to manipulate things, to refashion the world. A God complex, not as overwhelming as the President's, but still, there it is. And most of them do, in their very private hearts and souls, dream of taking that oath." He shook his head again. "But, you see, that doesn't explain scientists. They don't have the urge, the need to manipulate people and use power. Most of them live in a world unpeopled, without power, and desire nothing more than to be left alone. What is it?"

"Grange, then, according to your definition, isn't a scientist as much as he is a politician."

"True. He's the breed of scientist that scares me shitless. This new scientist," he said, "wants what the politician has always wanted, but he is going about getting it in a different way, not through the pacification of the public with panaceas, the way we have to do it. He doesn't give a damn about the public. He is getting it through us. We're the subjects that he is manipulating to get what he wants. And we're helpless to prevent it. I studied law, for God's sake! What do I know about physics? Or biology? Or psychology and conditioning? It's their world now. The scientists' world. They know it. They made it, they understand it, and they know what they want to do with it. They can change it or not, make it better or worse, blow it right to hell. And we don't even know what they're talking about. All we do is give them money and pray."

Peter waited. He never had seen Ed so bitter.

"Goddamn it, how can I question Grange? I don't know enough to question him. What the hell difference does it make when someone like Poole says science is apolitical? Is Grange apolitical? When he gets the power he wants, will he use it apolitically? A man like Grange, brilliant, gifted, he can keep up with my world without any trouble. And I have to be totally ignorant about his. I just don't have the time, or the kind of intelligence, to let me understand what he's doing, why, what he hopes to accomplish. My world, the political scene, must be like kindergarten stuff to such a man. How contemptuous he must be of anyone who isn't a scientist. And his field is just one of the specialties. Every science you can name has its own Grange pushing for something that is as esoteric to the laymen as anything in Grimm's world." A note of self-pity had entered his voice; abruptly he stopped, and his hand rested heavily on the briefcase, bulging with unread material.

"Leave that stuff with me," Peter said. "Let me glance over it. I have plenty of time, and you need some sleep."

Chapter 7

Ed didn't disturb Lil when he got into bed. It had gone
sour, with no reprieve in sight, and they both knew it. Not
mean, hurtful viciousness, à la *Virginia Woolf*, but sour.
He should take the guest room and be done with it, but
what would the kids think? It would get out, back to
Pennsylvania, rumors of divorce, ugly stories. Nothing to
them, but make the son of a bitch deny it. If he reached for
her, she wouldn't deny him. The groping in the dark, the
sleepy acquiescence, the taste of wet kisses. Passionless,
but not denied and never mentioned. That summed up
their lovemaking. Ed put his hands under his head and
stared at the pale oblong of the window. He thought
about Dr. Krump and what he had said.

"The amnesia was total, you realize. He had to relearn
everything, from control of his bladder, to how to walk, to
how to speak and read. Everything. You never knew how
much the brain can adapt until you start on such a
program. Usually there is a great loss of abilities. Your
brother has been most fortunate in that respect."

"But he isn't well. That headache he had! And his side
was paralyzed. The whole left side!"

"But is isn't paralyzed at other times." Krump had
squeezed him in between patients; he was impatient for
him to be gone again, but he didn't obviously hasten the
end of the interview. "Senator, I know how frustrating all
this must be, to you, your wife, most of all to Peter.
Frankly, we don't know what to expect next. All we can
do is keep an eye on him. Few people with the massive
damage that he suffered could have come this far. We are
hopeful for him. If there is any measurable change in any
of his tests, then we'll have something to work with."

Ed had stood up then, knowing it was futile to press it,

angry that he had learned nothing more than he already knew. At the door he hesitated, wanting to ask once more for some reassurance, then he shrugged. "Thank you for seeing me."

"I am sorry, Senator. I wish I could have been of more help. I honestly can't recommend him for employment at this time, although if he took a job, or decided to go back to school, he just might do fine. But I don't know."

Ed looked at him blankly. "Has he asked for such a recommendation?"

"Not directly. I had a call from someone..." He shut his eyes, then opened them again. "Yes. Norman Pryor, checking a story that Peter had applied for a government position of some sort. Of course, I told him nothing. If there is an official request for his medical condition and history, I can only say what I have already told you."

Ed stared, feeling at a loss. Pryor? Why? He asked, "Did Norman Pryor call himself, not one of his staff?"

"Yes." Krump was tapping one finger on the arm of his chair.

Ed left a moment later, still puzzling about Pryor. A fishing expedition, but for what? In the downstairs lobby he saw a pay phone and stopped there and called Grange.

Grange's voice was smooth and unworried. "There's nothing he can find, is there, Ed? Peter is clean, isn't he?"

"You know he is. But what if he tries to get to me through Peter somehow?"

"Let's think about it, Ed. And meanwhile, keep Peter close by. Give him a job or something. Right?"

The oblong that was the window was growing, then contracting, and he closed his eyes; his body was too heavy, too detached for him to move now. He sighed once, and one of his hands came out from under his head and lay loosely on the covers.

The elevator descended slowly, passing pale gray oblongs without a sound, one after another. Ed fell asleep on the elevator and awakened to find that it was still descending. He was refreshed, and knew that he had slept for a long time. The air smelled clean and pure, and was pleasantly cool, not at all what he had expected. A light flashed on and off: Prepare to stop. He looked around, but there was nothing to do, no rail to hold, or chair to fasten himself to, so he merely waited, and the cage stopped without a bump or quiver. The oblong opened and he stepped out.

City street. No sky, not a real sky anyway, but an expanse of grayed blue, with real-looking clouds. The buildings were of a uniform height, seven or eight stories each, gray, with no windows. A moving sidewalk was densely packed with silent people, none of them looking at him, but giving the impression of following his movements with awareness. As he moved toward them a space opened, although none of them looked up. He mounted the first step leading to the movable walks, and found that the stairs were on the move also. There were three of them, and then he was one of the crowd going along effortlessly. His clothes were wrong, he thought. Too bright. He should be wearing gray. And his skin was too tanned and healthy-looking. His eyes weren't blank enough. He knew with despair that he wouldn't be able to pass after all.

He had been alone; now Lil was with him. She looked about grimly. "And what about me? What am I supposed to do here?" They were before a gray metal desk, a uniformed man behind it.

"What is your occupation?"

"I'm a housewife and mother."

"Insufficient to qualify. Next." The man in gray didn't look up at her. He tore a slip of paper in half and fed the pieces into a slot on his desk. Lil shrieked, but he didn't look up.

"She's my wife."

"Oh. Occupation?"

"United States Senator. Senator Roos."

"Both of you. First door to the left. Next."

Peter, who was there also now, or perhaps had been from the beginning, grinned at his brother and made a circular motion with his forefinger. "No occupation," he said.

"Student?"

"No."

"Insufficient . . ."

"He's a veteran."

"Reservist?"

"Nope," Peter said cheerfully.

"Insufficient to qualify." The man tore the paper, and put the pieces down the slot. "Next."

"No!" Ed said. "No! No! No!" His dream voice yelling hoarsely woke him up.

The oblong shimmied and became a window, and Ed sat up. He got out of bed quietly.

The light was still on in the study. Peter was there staring into the fire that had burned low. He had a lined yellow note pad on his knees. He was trying hard not to look at the sketch he had been making on it. Somehow the sketch was important to him, and he didn't understand why, or why he had made it, or what it was supposed to represent. He looked from the fire to his hands and then back to the hissing flames. The sketch was a city scene with block buildings, about seven or eight stories, windowless. Clouds rode in an artificial sky.

Grange's underground city, he knew, and he stared at it. Not merely an underground defense installation, but an entire city, and it was Grange's. He stared at it until he heard Ed's steps in the hall outside the door.

"Fast night," Ed said, entering the study.

Peter put the notepad down and felt the coffeepot. "Still hot. You should go back to bed, try to sleep a couple more hours."

Ed was staring at the drawing. The air was electric; he moistened his lips and looked up at Peter who looked at it, too, in puzzlement. Abruptly Ed closed his eyes and shook his head. He shuddered violently. "Freezing cold," he said and poked at the fire. "I want some coffee, then I'll read a while." His voice was hoarse.

"I finished with that bunch of articles you had," Peter said. "Made notes. Didn't want to get the typewriter out in the middle of the night. What they say in essence is that no one knows yet what to expect when they begin to gouge out the earth on that large a scale. They'll wait for the analyses of the reports from Colorado and Nevada to come through before they do more than surmise. Poole expects the worst: tremors, quakes, displacement of subterranean watercourses with possibly disastrous results, and so on. Also, he is violently alarmed about the thought of what would happen to the surface of earth if so much money got tied up in this scheme. I jotted it all down. Grange says nonsense. The problems are such that construction people can handle them all routinely. That's the gist."

Ed nodded. He rubbed his eyes hard, then sipped the steaming black coffee. "Yechh." He put down the cup. "In a minute I'll make some fresh coffee." He stared at the fire. "I had the damnedest dream," he said. "Don't you miss dreaming?"

"Yes. But probably there's compensation. They tell me that roughly every ninety minutes a sleeper goes into REM sleep. That's rapid eye movement sleep, when dreaming takes place. It seems that I have a pattern on the EEG that isn't too unlike that. Some kind of different psychic activity is taking place. One of the psychologists worked at making me believe that I at least hallucinate then, or black out, or something. If so, I'm not aware of it." He shrugged. "Interesting field right now, the study of dreams. Seems Freud was wrong in his belief that we dream in order to prolong sleep. Rather the reverse appears true: we sleep in order to dream. An integrative function of the mind, keeps us healthy, etcetera, etcetera."

Ed started to speak of his dream, then closed his mouth again, and instead picked up the coffeepot. "Be back in a second."

Chapter 8

Peter took D. C. to the school concert, and afterward they went home with Janice and Tom Knute for coffee.

"I'm sorry the concert made you uncomfortable," Janice said, pouring. "The acoustics were dreadful. And the kids are pretty bad, aren't they? The things we do so their memories of childhood will be good."

Quiet elegance, those were the key words, Peter thought, to describe their house. Simplicity that comes very high. Accustomed enough to wealth to accept it without thought, to be eccentric, or not, without the eccentricity becoming a means to prove anything. It just was. One wall of the room was covered with children's drawings, not particularly gifted artists, but there because Janice had liked them, and loved the children. Among the children's art were several paintings by Tom, and these were forceful and alive, and very good.

Tom Knute handed him a tiny, fragile glass half filled with amber liquid. "Try this. A Turkish coffee liqueur. I never can remember the name without reading it off the label, but we like it."

The talk rambled easily, pleasantly. It was light and comfortable. Janice mentioned the speeches Tom had made pushing for very strict environmental controls.

"Do you really think there's any point in trying to talk people into changing?" Peter asked. "Can change be talked into being?"

"You mean Ed and me, others in the Congress? Preachers?"

"For openers, yes."

"We have to believe it. First the talk, the exchange of ideas, then the laws, or the implementation of the ideas. Talk, always talk."

"And basically not much change. Laws get changed, the people stay pretty much the same."

"I don't agree. We have less tyranny now than at any time in the recorded past. More institutional concern for the well-being of the people..."

Peter shook his head to forestall a speech. "We still have tyranny, not from the palace, but from the laboratories, the schools, the courts, government bureaus right down to town commissioner. I just don't think people change. Only their institutions do. They'll follow a Hitler tomorrow, just as they did yesterday. What scares me is that what the great leaders did in the past was purely intuitive, and now this whole area is becoming understood, controlled, predictable. The behavioral branches of psychology are so accessible, the people are so susceptible, that's what is frightening. Reason," he added drily, "isn't one of the major tools they use."

"And it's the only one I know how to use," Tom said softly. "If I agreed with you, really thought it was a waste of time, then I would have to quit. Don't you see? You can't devote your life to a cause that you have no faith in. And if enough of us who do believe lost faith, then we'd lose everything by default."

Like Ed, Peter thought gloomily. Ed had lost faith. He said, "Coming back to the world after several years away, you can see things that we all accept without thought when we live with them day by day. I feel almost as if we're living in a confined area where one mechanical monster after another is being activated, each with the power to activate others. Sooner or later we'll be crushed by them, simply through their numbers, not through malice, or premeditation, just by being there. We can turn them off now, but later? I don't think so. I just don't believe the gentlemen's club of Congress can cope with them at the rate they're going. They're still trying to govern a world that died in the forties or fifties." And Tom, Peter thought, had no real awareness of the acceleration of the changes. Less even than Ed, who was aware enough to be very frightened.

Tom leaned forward and said, "Peter, you don't

understand how this government functions. We fumble the ball time and again. We delay. We let things go undone. But in the long run, we go where the people want to go, and what they really want is a better world. That's the gospel I believe in. I have to believe it. You're asking me if I believe in it strongly enough, and I have to say I don't know. I just don't know. But I don't dare not believe in it in spite of that doubt."

Janice shivered and one hand seemed to creep to her belly.

While Tom and Janice exchanged looks, D. C. touched Peter's arm and signaled time to leave. The good-byes were brief, as it is with friends who know they will be together again soon.

Peter felt vaguely upset, nervous, jumpy without a specific cause. Something about Tom Knute, he thought. Something about his mournful face, his sad eyes, and the way he lighted up when he looked at his wife. The way he had looked at him, Peter, with understanding, maybe compassion. He thought that Tom Knute was probably a very good man. He helped D. C. inside the car, Lil's Buick, and got in behind the wheel. They talked very little on the way to D. C.'s apartment. As he parked the car before her building, Peter said, "Isn't this your long weekend coming up? I'd like for you to come with me to Pennsylvania, the old farm there. Where Ed and I grew up."

She was silent for several seconds. Then, "Is there anyone there? Is the house open?"

"Mom and Dad keep it up. They spend their summers there. We all have keys. It'll be cold, but there's always coal, or at least wood for the fireplaces. We'd have to take food."

Again she hesitated, but then said, "All right. But I won't sleep with you." Peter nodded. "What kind of clothes should I take?"

"Warm things, high boots. It's about an eight-hour drive. We'll have dinner on the road somewhere, then go up. Okay?"

"Okay. I'll make a shopping list."

Later that night he wondered about his sudden compulsion to return to the farmhouse, and he became impatient with himself for questioning. It was important. That was enough.

There was a thick cloud cover when he picked up D. C. early Saturday morning. They would get snow later. He hoped not so much that they wouldn't be able to keep going. Neither mentioned it.

"You're really not going to quiz me, are you?" D. C. asked almost an hour later, breaking a long silence.

"No. Why? Should I?"

"Like I said before, you're not easy." She took a deep breath, then said, "M.A. Penn State, four years ago. Political Science. Joined the Senator's staff following graduation. Unmarried, twenty-six. One broken engagement three years ago. He broke it. Not especially interested in forming new alliances. Interested in Rodin. Enjoy canoeing, sailing, swimming, hiking, not much of a dancer. Drink very little. Like ballet." She stopped and looked at him without shifting her head more than a fraction of an inch.

"All right," he said.

"Oh, God. All right! I can't begin to understand you, Peter Roos. Okay. You win. Look there's a sign for a shopping center." They shopped, then drove again. It began to snow.

"Is it likely to snow too much to get to the farm tonight?" she asked.

"I don't think so. Less than four hours now. We have good snow crews in these parts. We'll tail a snowplow probably."

After lunch he drove slowly, seldom going above twenty miles an hour. It was a white world, bounded by a circular wall that kept them neatly centered fifty feet from any part of it. They followed a snowplow the last hour. At the farm driveway the driver cleared a pull-off space for the car, and they walked through hip-deep snow to the old frame farmhouse.

Chapter 9

"Eight, nine years ago my sister Nancy found this stove," Peter said, putting sticks in it. "She talked Mom and Dad into getting rid of the electric one and installing it. That was the year of the Cuban crisis. Ed advised them to build a bomb shelter out under the barn. It's still stocked with tuna fish and peaches and crackers." He glanced at her, but her face was unreadable. He added more sticks to the fire. The stove was an iron wood-burning range that filled one wall of the kitchen, with warming ovens and a mammoth bake oven and six burners. There was a poker hanging from the side of it, and blue porcelain tiles with raised designs decorated the front. "While this is heating up, we'll do the living-room fireplace."

He got another kerosene lamp burning. D. C. was shivering violently. "God, you're freezing, aren't you? Curl yourself around the stove. The kitchen will warm up fairly fast. I'll get the fireplace going and then tackle the furnace." He continued to talk to her as he went through the hallway into the living room. The house was as cold as the outside air, ten degrees, fifteen maybe. Neither of them had taken off any of their warm outerwear, but Peter felt comfortable, perspiring even, as he dumped an armload of logs on the hearth, and then put the lamp down on the old oak table that they had cut down for a coffee table. For a moment he stood quietly, looking at the room, and more free-floating memories became anchored, became his. Nothing had changed. Green and brown furniture, beige rug with a worn Sarouk before the couch. Green drapes drawn together. Little that was personal remained, that was the only difference. The tables had been loaded with cut-glass candy dishes, and monogrammed ashtrays, and gold-framed studio portraits of the girls, the grandchildren, a matched set of his mother and father, each looking away from the other. He wondered that no one had paid enough attention to their pictures to see that they should have been reversed.

"Peter, do you need any help?"

"No. Be through in a couple of minutes."

From the past came another voice: "Peter, are you playing in the fire again?" His mother had been in the kitchen; he had been sitting tailor fashion on the hearth.

"No." Carefully he positioned another piece of the candy wrapper and watched it erupt into a copper blue flame, then curl up, black and white, and crumble. No pause between the stages. One movement from wholeness to ash. The rain was still falling steadily. He turned and looked out the window across the room at the strange world. Rain on snow, melting windows, running down forever, sheets of water overflowing the gutters that were filled with snow and ice, a curtain of gray that didn't conceal the world, but distorted it further.

There had been four feet of snow on the ground when the rain started, a January thaw. For three days the weather had been mild and the rain steady. The New Year's Day blizzard had built hills and had filled in valleys; it had covered the low bushes and had made white chimneys of trees; it had frozen the river and made it one with the land, and now everything was being coated with flowing aluminum. When the skies thinned and the sun shone briefly, the dull metal became brilliant, eye-hurting silver, but the clouds regrouped and the glare was gone.

Ed and Peter had gone to town earlier. Ed had been restless and wanted to see the brook, and the swollen river that was climbing up the bridge. He bought cigarettes, candy for Peter, and they went home. Peter was thinking of the water and watching the paper wrappers burn when the phone call came. Ed was upstairs, studying, he said, but really to smoke. Their mother wouldn't let him smoke downstairs. Everyone pretended he didn't smoke at all.

Peter listened to his father's heavy voice, deep, like a record player with only the bass turned on, rumbling, vibrating. He hung up and said something to Peter's mother.

"You can't go over there alone," she said. She had a shaky voice, high and unsteady as if she were always afraid that what she was going to say might be wrong, and she was ready to stop any second and turn the rest of the thought into a laugh that was too shrill and began and ended in her mouth.

His father was on the phone again. "John? Listen, there's been a cave-in over at Upton Mine. Yeah, Goddamnit, they're down there! I don't know no more than I just told you. Get over here! I'm on my way there now. You wait here, you hear me? Just sit tight until I come back or call. Goddamnit, you do what I say! Just sit on your fat ass and wait for the word."

He stomped up the stairs and in a few moments was back down with Ed. They both looked sick, or frightened.

Peter added logs to the fire. He remembered the day Ed had taken him to see Upton Mine at Lincoln Township, between Scranton and Carbondale. Except there had been no Upton Mine any longer. There was an incline of ash and rock hills, and the remains of dirt roads that were being erased by gulleys and the intrusion of private garbage piles.

It was a summer day, windless, cloudless, and the air stank there. Sulfur, methane, rotting garbage. Strands of yellow-gray smoke rose from several spots, tenuous, unwavering ribbons twenty feet high that were then caught by an air current not noticeable on the ground that bent them toward the east, where they faded from sight. Nightmare landscape. The very beginning, or very end, of Earth.

"What's causing the smoke?"

"The old mine's on fire underground."

"Why don't they put it out?"

"They thought they had twice so far. But it just goes right on burning."

They tramped over the smouldering ground, forbidden ground. "Ed, do they have to evacuate the whole

Goddamned town? Can't they pump in water or something?"

"Watch your mouth, kid. Dad'll flatten you if he hears you talk like that."

The air was foul and he was glad when they left the valley and started to climb the hill to the town. The air wasn't any better. The mine was burning under the town; the ground was sinking in, gradually, hardly even noticeable as yet. But they didn't know how to put out the fire, and the people had to leave.

Peter stirred as the vivid memory faded once more. Eliot Noble had kept it from erupting into a major scandal, he realized for the first time. Good old Senator Noble, Ed's mentor in Congress, the friend of the family. And he thought suddenly how the family business had prospered during the past ten years. The construction firm his father and his uncle owned was a rich one, and he wondered, if anyone looked closely into it, would he find that much of their business was with the government. He shook his head hard. These weren't the memories he had come home searching for. Peter watched the fire for a few minutes longer, then put the screen in place and returned to the kitchen. The fragrance of coffee was overwhelming. The kitchen was losing some of the chill. Still too cold to take off coats and gloves, but no longer cold enough to give them frostbite where they were exposed.

"Furnace next," he said.

When he returned from the basement, D. C. still had her coat on, but it was unbuttoned now, and she was finding pots and skillets in the cabinets.

"Scrambled eggs, cheese, hot bread, wine, coming up," D. C. said. "How can you tell when the stove's ready to use?"

"It's ready. But if you have any doubts, a drop of water on the burner will tell. It'll skip about before it evaporates. If you're in a hurry, you can take the burner off and cook right over the flames, but Mom will be furious with you if you do that. It gets her pots too black."

"Oh. Well, we certainly don't want to make Mom

furious." D. C. put the skillet on the solid burner, and added a lump of butter.

You never could predict what might make her furious, Peter thought. He remembered her shrill, uncertain voice: "We flew to Japan while you were in the hospital, you know. They told you, didn't they? We stayed in a hotel for three weeks, and every day we waited in the waiting room. And you never woke up."

"Son, John says he has an opening for you as soon as you want it. R and D work, just up your alley."

"I'll let him know, Dad. Thanks."

"But what should I tell him? A couple of months? A week or two?"

"I'm not sure yet. I'll just have to let him know."

"Peter, don't use that tone on your father! He wants to help you."

The eggs were browned slightly, and the bread had a burned bottom crust. Peter and D. C. carried everything to the living room. It was delicious. They smiled at each other, warm and content before the fire.

"I'm afraid I was optimistic about the bedrooms being warm enough this soon. When you want to turn in I'll bring down some covers and stuff and fix the couch for you in front of the fire. Okay?"

"Whatever you say."

Later he started up the stairs to bring down the bedding, and she followed him. She was carrying the lamp. At the top of the stairs he let her go first.

"Ed's room was the one on the right, the last one," he said abruptly. She looked startled, then turned and walked quickly down the hall, went inside Ed's room and closed the door after her. Peter's hands knew where the linen closet was, and without thinking, he got out sheets, blankets, a couple of pillows and some towels. He left her upstairs and went to the living room, where he made up the couch for her.

She slept quietly, her breathing deep and slow, nearly inaudible. Nothing of her was visible except her hair, which gleamed in the firelight. Peter looked at the shining hair for a long time, then turned again to the fire. For a long time she had been tense and unable to relax, until she believed that he had fallen asleep in the chair, his feet crossed on the brown damask-covered hassock.

His mother's small face seemed to gaze at him from an appearing point between him and the fire. He studied her features, as one might examine a stranger. Small face, everything squeezed close together. As a girl's it probably had been sweet, as a woman's face, it wasn't. Baby-doll face with a lot of forehead nicely rounded, small pointed chin, scant eyebrows that she penciled when she went out, but didn't bother with at home, consequently she never became very expert with her eyebrow pencil and it was never certain what expression her brows would give her from one time to the next. When she began to fade everything went fast, and, overnight it seemed, she became an old woman with a pinched, pained expression, deep vertical lines between her eyebrows, along her nose, as if there weren't room enough for the development of wrinkles; they had to run up and down. Her eyes were always deepset and now they were so sunken that they appeared lidless, birdlike.

"Peter, you know you brother is an important man now. We all have to keep in mind that our actions might reflect back on him."

"Mom, get to the point."

She couldn't get to the point directly. There was a psychological maze that she had to run before she could approach the point. He hardly listened to her long involved windup. Finally she said, "You have to do something that is responsible. You can go back to school, of course. Or work for your Uncle John. Or teach. There are so many things open to you. A veteran, wounded, medals..."

"Mom, wait a minute, will you? First, I am not a hero. I wasn't wounded in that sense. I had an accident. It was caused by a foul-up. Our foul-up. A part fell off a helicopter and we crashed. One of our antipersonnel missiles went off. Our own missile killed three guys and wounded me. I wasn't even a part of the crew. A passenger, for Christ's sake!" He pronounced each word separately, forming the sounds precisely. She couldn't hear the words.

He thought of school. There was a rubber tree behind the water tower. One day a parent found it and complained bitterly and with horror. The groundskeeper was ordered to erect a fence around the tree and to inspect it personally each morning and remove any overnight blossoms. The students watched him to see how he would remove the evidence of cautious lust. He was a clever man. He brought a grocer's claw out with him and used that.

Lucy and Peter walked around campus talking. She wasn't pretty exactly but she had so much vitality that she gave the illusion of prettiness. She was small and muscular and quick in all her movements. She said, "Grange won't accept my dissertation, naturally. And after that, I just don't know."

"Why do you say that about Grange?"

She simply smiled. "But you're in. You and Simon if no one else."

Lucy had fine down all over her body. When he ran his hand over her, not touching her skin at all, but only the downy growth, she became goose bumpy and each tiny hair stood alone. Her breasts were firm and small and beautifully shaped, with rather large nipples, dark red, almost brown. There was a birthmark under her left breast, the size of a quarter, the color of her cheeks when she blushed. She said it was insensitive, but when he kissed her there, her nipples got hard and she caught her breath in a certain way. Her eyes were far apart and large, and her mouth was probably too big. She said of herself that she was all mouth and eyes. There was a slight gap between her upper front teeth, hardly noticeable in itself, but it gave her a look that would be always young and innocent.

Peter looked at D. C. resentfully. He should tear off the blanket, strip her naked and fuck the hell out of her, he thought. That's as close to a Roos ass as she'd ever get.

"When you're awake night after night, what do you do?" Ed's voice.

"Not much. Think, read, meditate. Walk, now and then. Write a little..." Indulge in a little self-abuse. You know how it is, Ed old buddy. You know how it is.

Chapter 10

The morning was brilliant, an eye-hurting glare everywhere. Peter made breakfast and as they ate, D. C. asked, "Why did you want to come here?"

He shrugged. "You know I had amnesia?" She nodded. "I had a crazy idea that if I came back here things would come alive again. The past. There are still gaps."

"Is it working?"

"I'm not sure," he said soberly. "Apparently filling in gaps proceeds with a randomness that is frustrating." And the past that he kept filling in was flat, meaningless, one-dimensional. D. C. was watching him. He said abruptly, "I'll take you tobogganing. I found our old toboggan in the garage, in good shape after all these years."

It was a good run. At first they seemed hardly to be moving, as if at any moment they might sink too deeply to move forward at all again, then so gradually that the acceleration wasn't noticeable, they picked up speed.

The first part of the run was one long curve, down from the barn, down and leftward to the beginning of the orchard where the snow was drifted five feet high in the open lanes before the rows of trees, making a natural banking curve that drew them on and down. As the end of the orchard came into sight, the trees began to slick by too fast to make them out as individual trees, but rather they merged into a wall of apparent solidity, and the wind was solid too, something they had to cut through with their faces, parting it forcibly. Their speed increased, the wind whistled and he thought D. C. screamed, but he couldn't really be certain. They hit each curve faster than the last, and then they were released from the ground, free, streaking with the wind and the snow and the sun and it was straight down all the way, faster and faster until the world blurred and only sensation remained.

Free as they flashed down the last slope, free as they entered the river at a bend, and followed it for fifty yards, free as they started the climb up a slope, leaving the river at yet another bend. Then the snow reasserted itself and the toboggan was reclaimed by the earth that dragged it to a stop finally in the cornfield.

For several seconds they sat not moving, D. C. pressed hard against Peter. Then she said quietly, "My God!" She glanced at him and moved away. "Another gap?"

Perhaps it had been his own scream remembered. Sitting in front between Ed's legs, feeling the strength of those legs as they held him securely, feeling a stranger in the world turned alien, with excitement building, building, becoming almost a terror not to be endured, except that those firm legs were a reassurance and even a promise, and he had believed in them, in Ed. The memory was as concrete as the wall of trees, and as false. He knew suddenly that he was desperately trying to reawaken that past, bring it into his present, and it was frozen back there, its attendant emotions as solidly encased in the past as if they had been living things overtaken by advancing ice floes, visible, and dead, to be looked at from a distance, but never rekindled, because the warmth needed to revive them would also make them dissolve and sink out of sight forever.

He began to work himself loose and the toboggan dug down into the snow. It was deep here, he knew from years past. The wind piled it up and the next day the wind tore it down. But it never tore down quite as much as it built up. When he got to his feet, he was in a drift that was nearly three feet high.

D. C. climbed off too, floundering almost instantly. She didn't sink as deeply as he did, and they began to climb back up to the house. Once she turned to look at the track they had made. "My God," she said again.

Then they were out of the drift and it was easier going. By the time they reached the house once more, they were both perspiring. Snow had packed into the zippers of D. C.'s boots and she couldn't undo them. Peter pulled them off. There was ice inside the boots, caked on the heavy wool socks he had found for her. When he worked them off, her feet were pink and warm. Her toes were bony and crooked, like her fingers. She stood up, stepped on ice, and squealed. He steadied her and for a moment they stood very close, his hand on her arm, her coat open, stocking cap still on. Her eyes were bright green against her pink face.

She sighed, hardly moving with it, "Just two people, no promises, no obligations." Her voice was little more than a whisper.

"No promises. Just two people who don't have a white whale to search for."

She smiled faintly and he kissed her. They drew apart and she opened her eyes slowly. He could feel her tension through the heavy outer garments. When he reached for her again, she stepped back.

"No more. I'll go fix one of the beds, get out of these pants. The snow's melting on them now." She turned and hurried out, in her bare feet. Peter took off his fleece-lined coat and his boots and socks, as full of ice as hers had been.

She had found his old room. The door was standing open and when he entered he saw that she had made the bed, using one of the great patchwork comforters his grandmother had quilted. It was drawn up to her chin. He undressed and started to pull the comforter down; she resisted a moment, then relaxed her hands and it came away. She continued to regard him steadily and soberly. For a moment he didn't move, then he caught his breath and let it go again.

"A real redhead," he said finally and looked at her face again. She lay without moving, her hands at her sides, and when he got in beside her and touched her, he seemed to release whatever had been holding the various parts together so rigidly. He kissed her deeply and kissed her nipples, and when his hand moved from her knee up her legs between her thighs, she opened her legs and the hot musky woman smell swept over him and there was no more thought.

Almost instantly afterward she sighed deeply and fell asleep. For a long time he didn't move, then he shifted gently, not awakening her, and pulled the cover over them. Her curiously ugly hand lay relaxed on his thigh.

They stayed inside, before the fire, the rest of the day. They played two games of chess; D. C. won the first, Peter the second.

"Are you going to join the Senator's staff?" she asked.

"I think not."

"He'll be disappointed. He's worried about you, Peter. And besides that, he needs you."

"I'll do some of the reading. I already told him that. But you know, and I know that he'll go along with the President. When has he not?"

"Would it be so bad, to put the defense facilities underground? And wouldn't it answer some of the criticism about using atomic energy for electrical power?"

Peter thought about Upton Mine, burning after twenty years. "Look, D. C., we can do it. God knows it could be done. But no one knows the consequences. No one. When they talk about gouging cubic miles out of the earth, no one knows what the earth will do in return. It isn't a giant potato that you can put a scoop to and hollow out here and there without having to think of consequences. If it were that inert, man wouldn't be so afraid of it."

D. C. threw her cigarette into the fire and watched it vanish among the flames. But men like Grange, she thought, aren't stupid. They know what they're doing, what the results would be.

"Men like Grange," Peter said bitterly, "know exactly what they are doing. Who do you think would have to run such an artificial environment? Who would be king, without the robes and crown maybe, but who would have the real power?"

D. C. felt frozen suddenly and a violent shiver ran through her.

"Why are you afraid suddenly?" he demanded harshly.

She shook her head. "I don't know. You've done that before, said what I was thinking."

Peter stared at her. And Ed. He had known a time or two what had crossed Ed's mind. And Bobby. And Lil. He rubbed his eyes hard. "You spoke about Grange," he said.

She shook her head. "I didn't. Peter... Let's make coffee." She jumped up and hurried from the room.

But she had spoken, Peter said again silently. She must have. After a moment he got up and joined her in the kitchen. D. C. hadn't started to make the coffee yet. She was standing at the window looking out at the white world.

Wordlessly Peter put the water on to boil, measured the coffee into the drip pot and got out mugs.

"You must have done something like that with Pryor," D. C. said. "You must have pulled something right out of his brain and startled him. All at once he's been all over the place asking questions about you, sending his people around, trying to dig out records."

"D. C., listen to me. Something happened to my hearing and that's all it is. Apparently I can hear things that are subvocalized, things that are inaudible to anyone else. It's rare, but there have been others."

She didn't turn from the window. "But only now and then? I've been subvocalizing at you since you came into the kitchen, could you hear any of it?"

The tea kettle whistled and he poured the water over the coffee. She whirled around, her face pale and set. "Peter, stay away from Pryor. All the way away from him, will you?"

"Jesus Christ! I said maybe six words to him! I thought he was your friend."

"He's nobody's friend. He can be dangerous, Peter. He would trample Jesus underfoot it if meant a story. And he's after you for something. I thought at first he was trying to get at Ed through you, but that isn't it. It didn't feel right, but this does. It's you he's after."

Chapter 11

They had coffee in the kitchen, and gradually D. C. relaxed again. From time to time Peter caught her watchful gaze on him. He told her about the accident, what he had been told about it. The accident was another blank.

"We crashed because of a half-assed repair job on the helicopter, and a drunk inspector who never got near it. I'm the only one who came out of it, three years ago, and I came out of it with my brain scrambled." He poured more coffee. "Still frightened?"

She shook her head. "I suppose I really was voicing my thoughts; you just spooked me."

"Right. Now your turn. Why did you come up with me?"

"To try to talk you into joining the staff. And to see if I could find out what Pryor was after. I was going to grill you this evening."

"Well, you know about the first. No. And the second, nothing. He couldn't be after anything. There isn't anything. Want to flip to see who does the steaks for dinner?"

She lost and burned the steaks. "From now on, I cook," Peter said.

"That's nothing. I can't sew either."

"Good thing for you you're pretty and good in bed," he said, cutting into the meat.

They went to bed early and after she fell asleep, Peter got up and sat before the fire and thought about the memories the house had revived. Unwanted, all of them. It had been a mistake. He had succeeded in making more of the past his own, and now it had the power to hurt again. It had all died once, a sudden death that was

74

without pain, a cessation so complete that there had been no clues to haunt him; knowing nothing, he had missed nothing. But what he was doing now had all the shock of deeply realized, unexpected bereavement. There was nothing back there that he could bring out whole.

He tried to think logically of what D. C. had said, that he had spoken her thoughts, and he could not keep it in mind long enough; it hovered on the edge of his awareness, slipped away again and again.

He thought about the classified ads he had found himself reading and knew that he wanted to leave Ed's house, be far enough away from him and Lil not to have to overhear their every word, know their plans and fears. He picked up the book he had brought and started to read. And early the next morning he and D. C. shut down the house and started back to the city.

Back in the assembly-line of Washington she said, "If you're really serious about moving out on your own, I know of an apartment in the building where I am. A friend of mine is getting married. She'd be glad to sublease it, I'm sure. Otherwise God only knows what you'll be able to find and when."

And outside her door she paused and said, "Did you tell him, the Senator, where you were going this weekend? That I was going with you?"

"No, I didn't mention it. He thinks I went to Harvard to look up some friends. Would you rather I didn't?"

"Yes. If you don't mind." She tightened her lips and withdrew herself so that she looked inviolable. She didn't shift her gaze until he nodded. "Thanks." She nodded toward the far end of the hall. "The other apartment is down there. Want to take a look? I have a key. Doris has moved in with her fiancé, but she didn't want to give this up until after the wedding. Parents, friends, you know. Her mail still comes here."

"It's fine," Peter said in the living room of the small apartment. There was a bedroom, a kitchenette, the living room, and a shower bath. The apartment was as impersonal as a hospital. Pale walls, off-white or faded beige. Rugs that were colorless. A three-quarter bed with a cheap blue spread. D. C. was talking about her friend; she'd taken everything that she wanted, the stuff in the apartment went with it. The living room had a small couch and a chair in the same faded upholstery; there was one lamp and an end table. A fragile desk finished the room. He was remembering another apartment, the one he had shared with Lucy in another lifetime. "*Naugahyde!* Baby, it's got *Naugahyde* chairs! Look! Blue leather. From a blue cow!" He shut his eyes hard and it went away. "It's fine. I'll take it if your friend is willing."

Peter got home to find Janice and Tom at Ed's house. They had had dinner, coffee was still hot.

"Would you like a drink, coffee?" Lil asked.

He said, "Thanks, don't get up. I'll help myself." As he poured coffee, he said, "By the way, I have an apartment. I saw D. C. tonight, and she knew of one in the same building that she's in."

Lil looked down at the drink in her hand. Ed's concern showed only in a quick puckering of his forehead, a quicker look toward Lil, back to Peter. "Trust D. C.," was all he said.

Tom had been talking about his reception at Columbia for a Lincoln memorial dinner. He came back to it with his drink in hand. "They didn't want to hear me," he said. "It wouldn't have mattered what I wanted to talk about, or who I was, nothing would have made any difference. They were ugly."

"You know that basically I'm in sympathy with them but," Ed said.

"Do you know how much it will cost to rebuild those dorms? The laboratories?" Lil said bitterly.

Peter wasn't paying much attention to them. He felt out of place, and wished he were in his own apartment already. Tom looked disturbed and Janice listened to something that none of the others could hear. Ed talked about a demonstration he had witnessed. ". . . whole new complex for *them*," Ed said. "And they acted like inmates rampaging against prison authority. . . ."

Peter visualized more and more buildings being erected, on a bed of corruption that was covered over with a plastic mat. The buildings were beautiful and functional and each was opened with great ceremony. But *they* hung back and wouldn't take part in the proceedings. And the corruption festered and grew and spread and presently it was oozing out from under the mat and the stench rose, and with it spores and germ cells, and like fungus or cancer, it attacked the loveliness above it and the oozing poison dotted the surfaces and the acids it produced ate away at the seams and the trim that slowly crumbled and putrified.... The bulldozers and the wrecking balls came in and flattened it all, sprayed it with deodorants and with growth retardants, spread more of the mats, treated this time to resist the incursion of the growth, and they started erecting newer buildings. But underneath it all the poisons waited....

Peter jerked away from the images, the fantasy. They weren't his fantasies, he thought, chilled, as he always was when this happened. But if not his, then whose? The others were listening to Tom now.

"... girl kept looking at me. She was plain, no makeup, no bra, you know the kind. But there was something so sad and so untouchable about her. She almost made me feel as if they do know something that we don't know or won't let ourselves know. They sense the corruption that underlies everything. Even if they are young and naïve. They know it's there, ready to leak out and touch them if they let it. They look at us and see it. I wanted to reach out and touch her, comfort her, but she wouldn't have allowed it."

Peter kept his gaze on the fire with great effort. The chill was deep and all-pervasive.

"You're tired," Lil snapped. "All they know is how to get a handout. Those saintly faces they put on are masks, Halloween masks they can put on or take off whenever it amuses them."

Peter got up then and stretched. "If you'll excuse me," he said. His voice sounded harsh to his own ears.

"Oh, Peter, you don't think I meant you! You're not one of them."

"I know," he said. Not one of them, not one of you. Not one of anything.

Chapter 12

D. C. knocked at his door at nine Wednesday night and sat crosslegged on his bed smoking for awhile. Except for two boxes of books, everything had been unpacked and put away.

"I had lunch today with Norman Pryor," she said. "He invited me."

"And?"

"I let him think that you had moved in here in order to be close to me. That we have a thing going." She stubbed out the cigarette.

Peter waited and when she didn't add any more, he said, "Doll, treat me like a corn shucker, right? I don't know nothing. From nothing. What Goddamn difference can it make if he thinks we have a thing going? Or why I'm here. Or anything else."

"Because if we have a thing going, then you're not here for any business reason. You're not working for the Senator. Or for Grange. Or with anyone else. You're simply captivated by my charms."

She hadn't looked at him as she spoke, but stared at the windows and the darkness of the night beyond. Peter felt helpless and stupid.

"Peter, he'll happen to come across you too, one of these days. It'll be accidental, probably. Just a chance meeting. He knows that we went to the farm, that you didn't go to Harvard. I don't know how he knows, but he does. He's really digging. Is there anything for him to find?"

"For God's sake, D. C.! What could there be?"

"I don't know. That's why I'm floundering about so."

The next morning Peter had a call from Gregory Grange. D. C. was finishing toast and coffee in his room when he took the call.

"Peter, my boy! For God's sake! I just heard that you're all right. I thought you were dead! Come over. This afternoon, four. Drinks, a few people. I can't tell you how pleased I am! For God's sake!"

Peter said he'd be there and hung up. He felt strangely disoriented in time, as if the intervening three years had dropped out of his life. Grange sounded exactly the same.

When he saw him that afternoon, he looked exactly the same. A vigorous fifty, only five eight, slight build, with bushy hair starting to gray at the top in a badger-like pattern. He greeted Peter with effusive delight.

"You're not well, are you? Something still not exactly right. No matter, you look fine. Better than you used to. More mature. More thoughtful. You were impetuous, weren't you, my boy? By God, it's good to see you!"

He introduced Peter to a handful of people in the hotel apartment, luxurious with a decorator look of impersonal good taste. All the time he kept a firm grip on Peter's arm. "Now, a drink. What? Scotch and soda? My drink. Peter, I tell you, that night when this came up, I paced all night wavering between advising you to spring for Canada or to go on in and trust us to get you back out. Then word came that you were critically wounded, that the prognosis was wretched. I relived that night many times, my boy. We tried to get you out, and we were too late. Well. Drink up, Peter. By God, it's good to see you!"

A young woman whose name Peter had already forgotten came up to them and started to talk to Grange about a speech he was to give at Antioch. Peter moved away. He realized that there would be no chance to talk to Grange here. A stooped man joined him at the side of the room. "Cocktail parties!" he said bitterly and drank.

Peter nodded.

"Marvin Dunlop," the man said and held out his hand. Peter identified himself and they became silent once more. He didn't know if Marvin Dunlop was someone he should know or not. He realized that Dunlop was watching Grange as closely as he was. Grange was standing by an attractive black-haired woman, talking to her with a smile. The woman shook her head, laughing.

"That's Mrs. Dunlop," the stooped man said, more bitterly. Grange was too close to the woman, and she was making no effort to back away. Peter finished his drink, put the glass down, and started toward the door.

"Peter!" Grange's voice was loud enough to stop the murmur of conversation in the room. He crossed the room, put his hand on Peter's arm. "Don't go yet. You must help me. This man, this person here, wants to do an article about me. Grange as teacher, isn't that the idea? Something of that sort?" The person who joined them was young, in his early twenties, and looked acutely embarrassed. Peter nodded to him. "It will be godawful, you know how that always goes, but still how can one refuse?" Grange said.

The hum of conversation picked up again, the clinking of glasses, a muted laugh. Peter felt Grange's probing gaze suddenly, and he felt also a contempt there, and a curiosity about him. The young man, he realized, was a plant, a ringer. This was the reason for his invitation to the cocktail party, to get him and this man together. This graduate student, he thought, and he looked quickly at the young man. He became aware in that moment that Grange's curiosity had abruptly deepened and sharpened. Something in Peter's face had aroused Grange's intuitions. It was all so quickly felt and sensed that Peter would have dismissed his thoughts as no more than a fleeting impression if Grange's attitude hadn't changed abruptly.

His voice became harder, the voice that Peter remembered from school when something had gone wrong, or someone had been an ass and not understood the first time around. "Never mind, Semple. Go eat something. You're pale, Peter."

"I have to go. Thanks." Peter didn't move, however. Grange nodded.

"I want to talk with you, Peter. Not here. Not like this. A quiet luncheon perhaps. I'll call you."

Peter felt frozen to the floor. It had happened again, he thought, and the chill hadn't warned him that it was happening this time. Nothing had warned him. Abruptly he turned and went to the closet where his coat had been hung. Grange didn't follow him, or see him out. He stood where he was, watching until the door cut off his view of Peter.

Peter was due at Ed's house for dinner, but he was in no hurry to get there; he walked for an hour, wondering at Grange's interest in him.

And even more, wondering what the hell was happening to him. Intuition, he said softly. His intuition had told him that Semple was a grad student, Grange's student.

"Isn't it wonderful," Grange had said once in his most acidulous voice, "how intuition works only after you have put in the donkeywork of gathering facts. How many laborers in the cotton fields ever came up with benzene rings?"

He finally hailed a taxi and was driven to Ed's house.

Mrs. Haines opened the door for him. They were in the study, she said. Even before he entered the study, Peter found himself bracing for bad news. It was in the air, and when he saw Lil and Ed, the feeling of things gone wrong increased.

"You don't know about Janice?" Lil said shrilly. "She's in the hospital! She was mugged today! Pushed down, her purse grabbed. Outside Children's Hospital."

Peter looked at Ed. "How bad is she?"

"We don't know yet."

"I told her that was a bad place. Filthy neighborhood. In the afternoon! It was in the afternoon!"

"Is one of their kids in the hospital?" Peter asked, ignoring Lil.

"No. No. She reads to the kids in the hospital three times a week. Has done it for years."

"Not safe to go out without a guard anymore. You can't go anywhere alone. I'm afraid to walk down our own street. Here! In this neighborhood! Where were the police, they's what I want to know. Where was her driver? Why did Tom let her go there alone?"

Ed's hand on her arm stopped her and she finished her drink. Abruptly she rose and left the room. "Terrified," Ed said. "She isn't the only one around here like that. It's ugly, and getting worse. I'm waiting for D. C. to call. She's trying to find out how badly Janice was injured." He closed his eyes and rubbed them hard. "I hope to God this won't keep Tom from the hearings next week."

"Have you decided?"

"There are inclinations, proclivities that you get to count on, you know. I suppose I'm not really opposed. Tom is, on principle. We need him for balance."

Peter sat down and tried not to think of Janice. "I saw Grange today," he said. For the first time he wondered how Grange had got his number. "Does he have the committee votes?"

"I don't know. Tom swings a lot of weight. He's highly respected and they listen to him. Without him? Christ! I don't know. Grange is a big man. Smart. Would he be sticking out his neck like this testifying for the bill if it wasn't a sure thing? And a good thing. What would be in it for him? What more could he want? And would it be much different than living in a modern building now? Air conditioning, elevators, stores, all self-contained. What's the difference?"

"Have you ever been in one of those modern buildings when the electricity went off? The windows are stationary; they won't open. At least you can walk down and get out, if you don't get crushed on the stairwells. But imagine having that happen a mile below ground. You'd suffocate before you could go from one level to another."

"Oh, don't talk like a child. That's bullshit. There'd be safeguards, auxiliary systems, emergency equipment. That's not what bothers me."

"Ed, you're not talking about a simple underground defense system, and you know it. You're talking about an entire city with an artificial environment that would have to be maintained at all costs. One mistake could wipe out everyone in such an environment. And the experts who would decide what was needed would be speaking a foreign language to the laymen. They are the ones who would have to make all decisions—the technicians, the engineers, the scientists. They would be in control, and the control would have to be absolute. I'm talking about control at the biological level, at the personality conditioning level. Possibly irreversible changes."

He was watching Ed and felt that his words were glancing off him. The wrong time to go into all that, he knew. Abruptly he fell silent and turned to look at a painting over the fireplace. It was Squaw Valley. The snow looked real and cold. He asked suddenly, "Have you given up skiing?"

Ed flushed, then glanced at the painting. "I don't go as much as I used to. It's a young man's sport," he said. He looked at Peter quickly, as if to gauge his reaction. And for that reason only Peter didn't believe him. "Look, Peter, there were rumors. I don't know how you got wind of them. But they do move, don't they? There wasn't anything to them. I never took a cent, never lobbied for any airline, and if they arranged for me to be the guest of anybody anywhere, it was without expectation of repayment. I knew nothing about any of that."

Peter stared at the painting. He couldn't bring himself to look at his brother just then. His question had been idle. He hadn't expected, or wanted a confession.

"Look," Ed said in a voice that was weary and somehow petulant, "nothing's simple anymore. It's the same old thing. You people have practically nothing to base your decisions on except your intuition, and to suggest that intuition isn't enough in this world means we, the rest of us, are turning a deaf ear. But dammit, it isn't enough. These installations. Basically it's a good idea to put below ground those things that are naturally dangerous and possible sources of pollution. All these hearings are for is to decide if we should look into it. Period. These problems you brought up, they'll be examined minutely, by experts in the various disciplines. No one is committed to anything, except to appropriate enough money for initial studies. How in God's name can you know whether it's good or bad before anyone comes up with thorough studies of the problems? It's like the SST. Its opponents just knew it was bad. Big revelation, I guess."

Peter watched him, fascinated by a change that had

come over Ed. Hardly noticeable at first, but now, toward the end of this speech, Ed's manner was that of a man before an audience. It happened often, Peter thought in surprise. Ed hid behind an invisible shield; his senatorial front protected him, no barbs could penetrate to the man, they would glide past him, glance off. He was talking about his duty now.

"... constituents know both sides. That's the purpose of the hearings. The people have a right..."

"Ed, this isn't *Face the Nation*," Peter said gently.

Ed looked sharply at him, then he flushed a deep red, and stood up. "It's a reflex," he said tiredly. "I even hear myself do it sometimes." He kicked at the fire, and watched the shower of sparks that he stirred up. "But, my God, Peter, it is not simple any more. It is not easy."

Peter remembered a hike with Ed, a long time ago, soon after Ed's return from Korea. They had gone up into the woods where the floor of the forest had been carpeted by pine and spruce needles. It was still and hot that day, and by the time they had reached a summit where they could rest and look down over the valley, they had been sweating heavily and for a long time they had not spoken. And then Ed had started to talk about the buildings he would create, functional, beautiful, designed for people, not for the business they carried on within them. Why hadn't he gone on into architecture then? But he knew. Their father, Uncle John, Senator Noble. Too much pressure to do something worthwhile. Too much scorn, implicit and explicit, for the effete artists who became architects. And Ed had yielded, had allowed himself to be molded, because it was simpler that way. They had always made Ed bear his burden of eldest child, first son, and he had accepted the role. Simpler? But for an hour on that hot day Ed had projected visions of graceful buildings, and Peter had shared them. Then the visions had faded.

Lil opened the door. "D. C.'s on the phone, dear."

Ed went to his office and Lil looked uncertainly at Peter for a moment, then excused herself again, murmuring something in a low voice. Her manner toward him was in flux. His attack had frightened and disturbed her, and she seemed afraid of him now. Afraid of being alone with him.

Peter wanted to leave before his brother returned, but he waited. How little they had to talk about any more, how near to arguing they were most of the time. They evaded it only because they both dreaded arguing with each other. Whatever had held them so close in the past was dissolving; the loss would be irretrievable.

Peter turned from the picture of Squaw Valley and sat down. How did he know intuitively the cities would be bad? How did he even know cities were being planned, not merely defense facilities? He remembered suddenly an ant farm that had been in Grange's office for months. "Look at the little bastards," Grange said. "Right there is a demonstration of how perfect cloning would work: each member is interchangeable with all others of its class. Just think what they could have accomplished if they hadn't been so rigid at the top. Hell! There is no top. They're all clones!" His gaze swept those students gathered in his office. "Our society is almost as rigid as theirs, the division of classes by intelligence; work or no work, poverty or riches, all decided by intelligence. But the system is so Goddamned flawed there is no security or satisfaction in any of the divisions. Low normals dream of becoming executives, and executives have nightmares of Skid Row. If intelligence was the criterion, and if intelligence was predetermined at birth, that, my fine friends, would be the real utopia."

Grange had done work on prison inmates; he had experimented with brain implants of electrodes, drug therapy, aversion conditioning. All in the past fifteen years. More recently he had worked in a hospital for dependent, retarded children, and never had published anything about his results. Peter wondered if Grange wouldn't consider an underground city just one more laboratory, bigger and better than ever, but no more than he deserved, with no outside supervision or interference. He suspected that no one but Grange himself knew how far his experiments had taken him. He knew that Grange had published little of importance in five years, and that during those years he had been very busy.

And the experts, Peter thought, who would be the opposing experts? Those who had much to gain from the project could gamble on the time and labor involved gathering data to reinforce their views. But the dissident voices? What would they gain? The time used for research would be time stolen from their jobs, their weekends. And if they did prevail, theirs would be a negative victory, with nothing to show for it except fatigue and possibly satisfaction, and the knowledge that the proponents would be back in a year, two years, ten. They always came back with bigger guns, more ammunition.

Ed returned, looking worried. "She's bad," he said. "They don't know yet how bad. Broken arm, shock. They may decide on a Caesarean." He scowled at Peter and said, "Maybe it wouldn't be all that bad, having a controlled society. At least everyone would be safe."

Chapter 13

Sunday afternoon Peter dropped in on D. C. in her apartment. "You want some home-cooked dinner tonight?"

"Like what?" She was wearing tight red pants and a sweater, no makeup on. Papers were spread on her desk.

"Black bean soup and sausages. I got carried away."

"Deal," she said.

Peter picked up a stack of photographs and began to leaf through them. She glanced at him, then turned again to the work she was doing. "Who are they?" he asked.

"Assorted creeps who'll be haunting the hearings next week. Some of them are with S.A.F.E., the underground paper."

Bearded young men, blue-jean-clad young women. He turned the pictures face down and looked at a group photograph. Young women, several of them circled. Suddenly one of the faces jumped out of the picture and nothing else existed for a long time. Short nose, long dark hair, not really pretty. Grinning lopsidedly, showing a slight gap between her front teeth. He turned the picture over and read the note on the back. Lucille Shofner, formerly Lucy Boardman. Co-founder of S.A.F.E. Washington address... Somehow he left D. C.'s apartment, found a cab, rode, got out again and walked. He walked slowly and his movements felt awkward, forced, his arm swinging too hard, his hand hitting his leg, feet too loud on the sidewalk, rigid shoulders. He felt as if every house on the block were shielding observers; they photographed him, noted his self-consciousness. He took a deep breath. Now his hand touched the spiked iron fence and he trailed his fingers over it. The lawn was tidy, symmetrical yews at the steps, a border of deep green ivy outlined the whitewashed foundation stones of the building. Venetian blinds covered the windows. He turned in at the gate. Just another two-story house, frame, like others all up and down the street. Taped to the door was a small sign: S.A.F.E.—Save America For Everyone. Another smaller notice told him to ring and walk in. He reached for the bell, then took the doorknob instead. He doubted that a bell could be heard; separated as he was by the door from the activities of the house, the noise level was almost unbearable. He opened the door and entered.

For a moment he hesitated, holding the door. Straight ahead twelve feet away was a staircase. Two girls stood talking to someone above them, out of Peter's sight. They wore high boots; one had a miniskirt, the other blue-striped jeans tucked into the tops of her boots. Both had very long straight hair, neither very dark. They finished the conversation and ran down the rest of the way, pulling on coats as they came. He moved aside and they ran out, banging the door. He was in a wide hallway, doors open on both sides, the stairs ahead and a continuation of the hall, darker and narrower. Telephones kept ringing, and typewriters clattered. A fragrance of baking bread was in the air. Music, radio and live guitars, voices, yelling, laughing, singing, talking. A group of five people clustered at one of the doorways, arguing with those inside the room. One of them, long-haired, blue jeans, noticed Peter and elbowed a tall black man standing next to him. He indicated the front door and the black man left them immediately and moved toward Peter. He didn't give an impression of hurrying but his stride was long and he wasted no motion.

"Anything I can do for you?" To his left in the end room a girl was wailing, "Speak up, I can't hear you."

"Lucy," Peter said. "I'm looking for Lucy Boardman, or Shofner."

The black man didn't move, but everything about him changed. His attitude of careful neutrality vanished; it was almost as if he radiated an instant wariness. Peter realized that this man knew who he was and hated him. The black man nodded, motioned Peter to follow him and went back into the shadowed hall. He opened a door without knocking, went inside and held the door open for Peter to enter.

"Lucille, baby, this here cat says he wants to see you."

There were people around a table. They had been reading from typed pages when the door opened and hadn't looked up. Now they did. Peter couldn't have said later if the others at the table had been men, women or baboons. She had been sitting with her back to him, her black hair glossy and heavy on her back. She turned, twisting her torso to see, her right hand tight on the back of her chair. Her eyes were enormous and seemed larger and darker as the color drained from her face. The man who had brought Peter here sucked in air and Peter thought, please God don't let him be Shofner. Please. Lucy stood up, pushing the chair, almost knocking it over. She caught it and broke the long locked stare.

"Peter, good God, what a shock!" Now twin pools of crimson spread over her cheeks. She laughed and put her hands to her face. Then she said very swiftly, "I'm in the middle here. Can you hang around? Are you in town for long?"

"Coffee break, Lucille," one of the men at the table said. He lighted a cigarette, keeping his eyes on Peter.

"You've met Carl, haven't you?" she said, indicating the black man. Peter shook his head. "Oh, Carl Davis. Peter Roos." She pointed at the people around the table and said their names. They inclined their heads, or smiled.

"Can I talk to you?"

She hesitated, then nodded and walked past him into the hall. The noise instantly isolated them from each other. Without looking back at him she led the way upstairs. He had forgotten how small she was. She wore a below-the-hips knit top over bell-bottom pants and nowhere did the clothes cling to reveal her body, but her delicate wrists and the slenderness of her neck and hands, the planes of her face gave her a look of fragility that was contradicted by the swift sureness of her walk.

The room she led him to was a bedroom, used as a cloakroom. The bed was piled high with coats, as was a chair and the chest of drawers. A line of boots stretched along the wall. There was a very narrow corridor for them to stand in. Lucy stopped and faced him.

"You never wrote."

"I would have eventually. I got the clipping, while I was still in training, the one saying you were gone, with a black activist. Carl?"

"You didn't even bother to ask if it was true."

"I would have. I did finally. I sent it in care of your parents, just before I shipped out. It came back. No forwarding address. I thought at first it was your handwriting. That was a dumb thing to do, no forwarding address. I wrote again."

"When was that?"

"In the fall. Last November."

Her face set in furious lines. It was as if they hadn't been apart. Face-to-face accusations, nothing held back, no fear of battle with each other. "Last November! You thought I'd still be sitting at home three years later! Move! I have work to do." She took a step toward him; he didn't move. "Why don't you give me your number, where I can reach..." Suddenly she stopped, her eyes were searching as she examined his face. "Peter, you've been hurt, haven't you? Hurt bad."

He nodded. "Who's Shofner?"

"My mother's maiden name. Are you all right now? Will you be all right?"

"I don't know." She took another step toward him, then another and he caught her and held her hard and too tight. "Lucy, Lucy," he whispered into her hair, unaware of what he was saying, and she wept against his chest. After a few moments he said, "We've got to get out of here. Someplace where I can touch you, look at you, where we can talk." She pulled away from him.

"Do you have a Kleenex? Oh, God, look at me."

He reached around her for Kleenex at the dressing table. She blew her nose, glanced in the mirror and shuddered. "Okay, let's go."

Carl was lounging at the foot of the stairs, reading or pretending to read a magazine. He glanced at Lucy, then fastened his gaze on Peter. His face was blank, his eyes flat and hard.

"I'm going out, Carl. Will you go over the rest of the copy for me?"

"Sure, baby." His gaze didn't waver. "You taking the car?"

She turned to Peter questioningly. "I don't have wheels," he said. Carl dug in his pocket and brought out keys on a chain with a silver peace symbol and tossed them to Lucy. "See ya, baby," he said, looking at Peter. As they went out the door, down the steps, through the iron gate, across the street Peter felt his hard-eyed stare on his back.

She still had the same Dodge she'd had before. Wordlessly she handed him the keys and went around to the passenger seat. He got behind the wheel, and didn't have to adjust the seat back. Someone had taped the metal end of the gear shift where the plastic knob had come off. He had always meant to do that.

A long time ago she had asked, "Do you believe in ghosts?"

"I'm not sure. Something maybe. Why?"

"I think places are haunted. You go in and something awful that happened there is waiting for you. It starts and goes through to the end every time and you just have to let it go. You can't stop it." She had been talking about her reception at home. Her parents had learned she was living with a man, with him. He knew what she meant. The car was haunted with their last scene. It waited for him and pounced as soon as the motor started.

"You're going! You're really going!"

Strangely he couldn't remember where they had been going; he had been driving south, he knew; the ocean had been to his right. Lucy leaned toward him. She wore patched blue jeans, gray sweatshirt, her hair was stringy because she'd had a cold for weeks and hadn't shampooed it. "You're really going, aren't you?" He could smell salt spray, and forest mold, and a faint lingering odor of camphor.

"You haven't heard a thing I've said, have you? Grange

says I should go while he's digging out my records. He'll fix it."

"Grange! Grange! Grange! What if he doesn't fix it? He won't be over there! You will be!"

"Lucy, for God's sake! What alternatives do I have? CO? They'd laugh at me. I filled out the application for appeal. Grange is going to add my school transcript, his own request that my deferment be honored, and so on. He'll vouch for me in every way. And the man does have some influence, you know."

She ignored the sarcasm. In a low voice she said, "Don't go."

"Will you be reasonable!" He clutched the steering wheel hard, so he wouldn't hit her. The surf was running wildly, waves swift and high and breaking with explosive cracks. There was a storm off shore. Don't go, he thought bitterly. "For crissake, will you tell me how not to go in?"

"Your brother."

"Can't do anything. I wouldn't ask him, but even if I did, all he'd be able to do would be to get me assigned to a fat officer in the Pentagon, something like that. Cozy."

"Canada."

"I won't run and hide. I have a legitimate deferment, for crissake. That'd be great for Ed back home. His brother a fugitive. Win a vote or two that way, yessirree. You know what Pennsylvania's like?"

"I don't give a shit what Pennsylvania's like! Or if he ever gets elected town crier!" She held his arm with both hands. "Peter, I'm afraid. Please, talk to someone who isn't one of Grange's men. Not his lawyer. Let's find someone not connected with the school and all."

"Why have you turned against Grange? Did he make a pass or something?"

She withdrew her hands, opened them wide, then closed them into fists. "Don't keep sidestepping. I don't trust him, that's all. Will you find someone else to talk to?"

He sighed. "Look, honey, he likes me. I'm doing some pretty heavy work for him. He doesn't want to lose me. Dig? I can see why you don't trust him. He's afraid of you.

He doesn't know how to act with women, and especially brilliant ones. I guess all his better female students feel uneasy with him. But there's no reason for me not to trust him."

"If you go, I won't wait!" she said it vehemently, with the sort of change of pace that always left him floundering a bit. "I'll go to Canada with you. Or hide in a cellar. Or wait forever at a prison gate. I'll help you fight it. Work to pay a lawyer for you. Anything. But I won't be here when you come back if you go."

"A few weeks at the most. Maybe a month."

"We'll be finished."

"Don't be so pigheaded. Someone made a mistake with my classification. This is the quickest, most painless, most private way of straightening it out. Grange will get me out in a few weeks. Don't make a big deal out of it."

"Sure, you'll be back, like Mel Stein."

"He had a breakdown. What's that got to do with anything?"

"That's what he said. A few weeks. A little rest, then I'll be back. Just like him."

He didn't understand how she could be so brilliant and so irrational at the same time. "Well, I'm not crazy," he said flatly.

"You are if you go."

"Lucy, I don't have to go until Monday. Let's go up to the mountains for the weekend."

"Hah! You don't believe me, do you? You think I'm kidding. I'll get over it. Just a little screwing will put things right and I'll send you cookies and a letter a day and keep the other cats out of my bed. Forget it! I'm moving out now. You can do what you want. I'm through!"

He tried to pull her to him and she hit him hard under the right eye. "Just go fuck yourself, soldier!" She was crying furiously now, and yanked open the door and stumbled from the car. The next day when he saw her, her hand was discolored and swollen. His cheek was cut. Neither spoke.

Did she remember it like that? She couldn't. She would

have got rid of the car. He drove and they were silent until he stopped near his apartment.

"Terribly respectable, isn't it?" she said, glancing up and down the street.

"Yes." He pushed the door open for her and they entered the lobby. "From my window, they tell me, you could see last summer's riots just fine." The elevator was there.

He watched her but she avoided his gaze deliberately, stood very stiff with her hands in her pockets, her shoulder bag pressed against her side. He began to feel as if this one trip would occupy his entire life. His apartment was on the ninth floor. Never had the elevator ground up so slowly. Then they walked and walked and walked down the hallway. Finally they were inside. She glanced about casually and moved to the window, and stood looking out.

He followed, then stopped in the middle of the room. He didn't know what to say to her, how to start it again. She seemed remote in a way that he wouldn't have believed possible. "I'll make coffee," he said.

"Don't bother, Peter. I'm not staying that long." She turned toward him. "Now that we're here, what's there to say? It's over. Our time ran out. We can't pick it up as if the last three years didn't happen. Even if we wanted to. We aren't those two people anymore. And I don't want to be her again."

"Why are you using your mother's name?"

"Dad kicked me out. Nothing's so respectable as a Kansas City optometrist, you know. Out, filth! Be gone, whore! You made your bed. Take your degenerate friends with you." She didn't even pretend that it hadn't hurt. "You know. That whole scene. I said, sure, I'll go, and you'll never be bothered by me again. Blah, blah, blah. Right on cue. Both of us. Mother, too, crying on the side. First at him. Then at me. Costumes by Sears. Lighting by God. Lines by Sally Smith, she's a freshman in her first creative writing course."

"Why?"

"Good old picky Peter. I was in a bust. In view of my record, my youth, Dad's lawyer, etcetera, etcetera, I got a suspended sentence and disciplinary probation from the dean." Suddenly she did smile. And there was that small space between her front teeth. Peter felt his legs turn watery. The pleasure-pain of desire was more pain than pleasure. "They raided the wrong place, wrong time. All they found was one lousy joint that Freddy was saving for Doris." Carelessly she added, "Carl was there. Identified by the press as a radical, a Panther, an activist, God knows what else. Nowhere was it mentioned that he was a Cornell history professor, Ph.D. and all."

"The degenerate friend? The one the clipping said you left with?"

Again she shrugged. It didn't matter. Nothing did. "That was three days after you left. About a month later I found some acid in my desk drawer at the lab, gratuitous, from an unknown admirer, no doubt. I flushed it down the toilet and in about thirty seconds the cops were all over the place. A tip. Someone was playing nasty with me. You know what it would have meant if they'd found the stuff? Me on probation, all that shit. I split. Did Grange send you the clipping?"

"It wasn't just like that. He wrote to say there'd been trouble and you'd left suddenly. He wanted to get in touch with you about your work, your plans. He thought I'd know where to find you."

"Sure." Lucy left the window to sit on the arm of the overstuffed chair. She still wore her coat, buttoned to her neck. "When were you hurt?"

"June, a month after I got there."

"After you were hurt, why didn't you write to me? My mother had my address then."

"I told you. As soon as I was able to, I wrote."

"November?" She looked chilled in spite of the coat. "How bad? Where?"

"Bad enough. Head."

"God! God!" She jumped up and returned to the window, hunching down inside her coat, her forehead on the glass. "God, what a fuck-up!"

Peter went to her this time and turned her around. "That just about sums it up." He kept his hands on her shoulders, and she made no movement to pull away. Her eyes were very large and dark and clear.

"I assume you have a bed in here. Or do we use the couch?" she said. Slowly she began to unbutton her coat.

There was no foreplay, no talk. They seized each other, paying no attention to the niceties, or the subtleties. And when they came together, they both wept without restraint. And then they could talk.

"You've filled out here a little."

"You're kidding. I lost three pounds. My clothes are all too loose."

"Your birthmark is darker, isn't it? Should it be getting darker?"

"I'm sure it isn't. Let me see the place on your head."

"What did you do with my ring?"

"I have it. I couldn't get it off to give it back before you left. My hand stayed swollen for almost two weeks. I think I chipped a bone."

"Poor baby."

"Don't be sarcastic."

He got up and made coffee and sandwiches and took them back to bed. They sat up, naked, eating and drinking and talking.

"Where's Simon?"

"Teaching high school science in Terre Haute."

"Simon?" Peter poured more coffee. "How about Mel Stein?"

"Never came back. Still in a hospital as far as I know. I'm not sure."

"And Gus Yardley?"

"Flunked out. Quit. He went haring off after a stripper or something. Sells cars, or insurance, or brushes. And George Wesselman is still with Grange. He hasn't finished his dissertation yet. Just hangs on. That's the six of us. His class of failures. Why, Peter? Why each and every one?"

Peter propped himself on his elbow and looked at her. "What about his other students? Maybe Grange needs a rest, not his students."

She shook her head. "Only us. His ill-starred class. He said that to Simon when he rejected his dissertation. His other classes are fine, graduating right and left, going into all kinds of great things." She lifted her coffee with both hands and looked into it. "The day I left, during the acid business, I sort of backed up toward the rear window. Remember how the room was arranged? My desk and Simon's at the rear, the windows on the long wall. The last casement window was open and it was a mirror, with the line of sight out of the door, down a bit to Grange's door. I saw him, Grange, across the hall in his doorway. He was just standing there, waiting, expecting something. After a few seconds he came across and paused at the door listening. Then he came in blustery and excited, what were they doing there, all that crap. But it was an act. I saw him. He was disappointed that I wasn't in tears, under arrest. Then Simon and George came in and there was a big argument over the warrant or lack of one, and things gradually went to hell."

Peter stared at her and she returned his gaze calmly. "You think Grange tried to shaft you? Why?"

"It always comes back to that. Why? I've gone over it a thousand times, convinced myself that I was crazy for thinking it, but it doesn't go away."

"They could have given him the word that there would be a raid that day. He might have pretended that he didn't know about it beforehand in that case."

She shook her head. "Someone had to have access to my desk. And I saw him. The look on his face. Impatient, aware. Nothing you could take to court, but I know what I believe."

"You know he's the star witness for this underground project."

"I know." A hardness came over her face, changing her subtly. "Peter, how did you know where to find me? What made you connect Lucille Shofner with me?"

He told her about the photographs. She bolted from

the bed and stood over him rigid with fury. He caught the dishes, her coffee cup, and put them on the bedside table.

"Jesus Christ!" Lucy cried, "They bug us, harass us every inch of the way, dog our footsteps, collect dossiers on us, plant agents. What are they so scared of?" She ran to the window and looked out, naked, not trying to conceal herself. "There's someone out there right now making a note of the address, my license, everything. Why? In God's name, why?"

"I don't know," Peter said. "I don't even know what you're doing. What you're into."

"A newspaper! We're printing the stories that none of the big papers will touch. And it scares them out of their skulls. We're going to cover these damn DEDF hearings. And they've already sicced their dogs on us, before we're even set up." She whirled around to face him. "You, Peter, where are you in all this?"

"I'm nowhere," he said slowly. "I was born last fall. What do I know?"

She continued to study him, and she changed again. She had decided that he was an unknown, Peter thought. He said, "Congress won't let them go ahead with it. From an economic viewpoint alone, it's suicide."

She shook her head. "If they decide to go through with it, they'll get the money. But you're right, it won't get done. The whole bloody mess will explode before then. Everything's boiling toward one big crisis. It'll blow. Pollution. Resources. Energy. Drugs. One day there'll be a traffic jam from Manhattan to downtown Washington, and fifty thousand people will die of carbon monoxide inhalation and that will be the signal for the final explosion. Or the famines will hit suddenly and we'll find little wars on a thousand fronts, and that will be the signal. Or something else."

She stood at the window as though transfixed, staring ahead. Peter caught her arm and drew her to the bed again. "You're shivering. You're chilled through and through." He held her, the covers pulled up over them both until she relaxed and no longer felt cold to touch.

Chapter 14

At nine-thirty they dressed and went out to eat at the Mexican restaurant that he liked. Hot peppery food, cold astringent beer. They returned to his apartment and bed.

Exhausted at last they lay close, not touching. Lucy's eyes were closed, she was pink all over. A faint smile lifted the corners of her mouth. "It's been such a long time," she said. "I'd almost forgotten this feeling, the third stage of lovemaking. God, I feel good!"

"I wish you could see yourself. You're like a postcard sunset—all colors that can't be real. Garish. Vulgar. Beautiful. Did you know your ears get red?"

"Maniac." She yawned and pulled the covers up. "I'm falling asleep," she said without opening her eyes, "And I can't yet. There's still something else." She yawned again. "There were others, Peter. While you were gone. I wanted to find someone else. I tried to. There were two. It didn't last. It wasn't like what we have. Nothing like. It was ... was sinful."

He laughed and she opened her eyes wide, blinked several times, then closed them again. "I've got to get up. Oh, Lord, I don't think I can stand yet."

"Stay, Lucy. Don't go."

"I have to. There's so much to do." She still didn't open her eyes, or make any motion to rise.

"Lucy, I have to check in for a routine exam tomorrow. They'll keep me overnight, I guess. They usually do. I won't see you again until Tuesday. Let me watch you sleep."

"Just routine?" she asked in a low voice, and now her stillness was tight, not relaxed at all.

"Routine. They do it every month. Go to sleep, honey. I'll get you up early."

She fell asleep holding his hand.

He watched her and memories swept him. They had had a big apartment, with six tall windows, a small bedroom, and a kitchenette, or something. It had appliances, a three burner stove, tiny refrigerator, sink. But it was actually one long room that was living room, study, dining room, dance hall, meeting room. The place was practically bare after their haranguing the landlord for weeks to remove the Naugahyde junk that had accumulated over many years of student use. They kept the bed, the kitchen stove and refrigerator and an overstuffed chair that Lucy covered with a red and white striped sheet. They used the chair creatively, she said once. Every bedroom should have such a chair.

They got liquor cartons, cut off the tops, painted them in primary colors and stood them on their sides, stacking them like blocks, and had bookshelves. They salvaged two slab doors and made desks, using glass blocks for the legs.

They cooked together, deriding their own failures, celebrating their successes with wine toasts, an inch or so of wine in the bottoms of sixteen-ounce glasses that she had found in a hardware store. They studied, pacing, muttering, completely ignoring each other when necessary. Sometimes she read aloud. Her voice was good, she might have been an actress: *The garden is, at present, only a square of naked earth, recently spaded, out of which are growing perhaps a dozen thin young orange trees a little shorter than a man, planted at A . . .'s orders.* Whenever she read aloud he ended up making love to her. Her voice was seductive; he was aroused watching a dimple form, vanish, reform at the corner of her mouth, watching the play of her cheek muscle as she spoke, the way she ran her hand under her hair in back, tossing it slightly as if it had tickled her neck. She regretted not having enough time to keep up her violin study. Sometimes she would take it from its case and polish it carefully, then replace it. Again she would start to play and hour after hour she would be lost to him. He stared at her as she played. Where was she? After such sessions she would be remote for a long time, only gradually returning to him and the world they shared.

There were other times when he felt only hostility for her, when they skirted each other carefully, or lashed out furiously, over nothings. She: "Why do you always wait until I'm all ready, then you decide you have to go to the john? Why can't you do it while I'm dressing? You have to make me wait to prove some dumb thing, don't you?"

"Why the shit don't you do one thing at a time? You never close a book or put a book away. You've got your desk and the table and the bed and my chair all filled with your crap."

"For crying out loud, will you just finish one beer before you open another one? Half-empty beer cans all over this dump."

"But you said you didn't want to go to the movie!"

"I didn't think we could afford it."

"How was I to know that's what the real message was?"

"You didn't want to know. You wanted to go out with Simon, didn't you? If you're tired of this arrangement, you can cut out anytime, you know! I'm not holding you down. No ties, buster."

It was as if at certain times a realization swept one or the other of them that a dependence had been allowed to grow, and the realization frightened them, made them defensive, or even resentful. Maybe the barometric pressure was too low at those times. Or too high. Or the moon phase was wrong. Or galactic masters with sensation rays were bombarding Earth then.

He watched her sleep. She slept so quietly, like a baby. He remembered lying on their bed, in their apartment. Naked, hot, ready for a shower. She had answered the phone, then handed it to him. As she walked away from him, he marveled at the baby smoothness of her buttocks. "What an ass!" he said fervently, hand over the mouthpiece. Then into the phone, "Hello."

"Peter, who answered?" It was Ed.

"My roommate," he said laughing, then unsuccessfully dodged a glass full of ice water. It got him in the crotch.

"Peter! Are you all right?"

That was when Peter realized what a decidedly dirty laugh she had. He couldn't remember what the call had been about. He remembered the letter that had come shortly after the call. "He hopes we'll be careful, not get ourselves in over our heads," he called to Lucy, who was stirring a pan of something that smelled garlicky. Another mistake. They masked most of their mistakes with lots of garlic, or wine, or both. "He hopes we won't end up with a house full of brats."

"Knock it off. He wouldn't say anything like that."

"That's what he means, anyway."

They had been in the middle of the marches and riots and protests. In the middle of, but separated from them by the excitement of being in Grange's class, of being together and needing nothing else. Seeing little else. "We had ours," he said softly. "We didn't give a shit for anything else." She didn't move. He wondered if he gave a shit now about anything. And he didn't know.

She had a lovely temper. Enough for both of them. He had read Ed's letter to her. "Who is she? Where is she from? Who are her people? What do you know about her?"

"That snob! What kind of clearance do I have to have to fuck a senator's brother? That son of a bitch! If I ever find out that he had me investigated I'll..."

Peter waited, interested. Abruptly she sat down and looked very small. "I won't do anything, will I? There wouldn't be a Goddamned thing I could do." He wondered if she ever thought of that day, that scene. Something cracked in her that day. A surface that had been sealed and glossed over and whole, impervious to anything she didn't care to know, showed a hairline crack that no filling or patching could erase again.

Later, when he answered Ed's letter, he wrote about her. Daughter of a Kanses City optometrist. Winner of a National Merit Scholarship. Pretty. His age. Ambitious. Smarter than he was. And really awfully pretty.

But she wasn't pretty in any conventional way. A beauty contest judge wouldn't even pause over her. Her face was so mobile, with fleeting expressions that sometimes made her seem very beautiful. At times she looked holy, until she smiled. But the slight gap in her teeth had simply made her more human, less angelic. That was good, he had said once, and she laughed when they came undone while he was trying to pull her to a sitting position from a prone position, without leaving her first. "Who could do this to an angel?" he said, pulling her to his lap and the expression on her face changed as she sucked in her breath and shut her eyes hard.

What had saved her from that emptiness of cinematic beauty had been her curiosity. Her large, dark eyes roved continually, always probing, searching. She could be a ferret, circling, forever coming back to an unanswered question, or avoided topic, giving it no rest at all until everyone else was wearied by her. She could cross-examine to the point of rudeness, unwilling to give up until a secret question that she never divulged was satisfied. Since he never knew exactly what that question was, he couldn't predict what it would take to answer it.

"Knock it off!" he yelled at her suddenly once, after answering the pointless questions long enough. "Don't grill me. No more third degree."

"What are you hiding? If you don't want to talk about it, just say so."

"Talk about what?" He took a deep breath. "We've gone over my preference for very hot bath water, that fact that I won't read a hardcover book in the tub. Life on the farm. Ed's wife's disposition. The case against lamb chops. For crissake are you writing an encyclopedia?"

"Don't be a real asshole, right? I was trying to decide if I'd ever marry you. I think not. Too short-tempered. Bad genetic material there. Your brother sounds like a prick. His wife's a winner, isn't she? And your old man. Whoopee! My father-in-law! Fat chance. I can't take a bath with you without getting cooked. And when I do bathe alone, you've used up all the hot water. And you spend more time on the john than a man should. I think you have a problem. But if you won't face it, then I wash my hands of the whole matter."

"I can't imagine why you hang around at all. Why don't you just piss off?"

"It's my apartment, is why."

"Crap! I found it! Ask the landlord whose name is in his book. Who pays the rent?"

Children, Peter thought. They had been simple, precocious children. Bickering, fighting, loving, stupid-blind kids.

He leaned back in the comfortable chair and closed his eyes. There was the gray city again, the gray people. Neat, orderly. Ten minutes under the ultraviolet light, scheduled for eleven A.M. She was in line. Her hair was cut short, flat against her skull. She really wasn't all that pretty. Her cheekbones were too prominent, her jawbones too sharp. She was thin, and her mouth was very large. Not pretty, but striking. He became aware of her docility, the vacant look in her big eyes that were not roving now, not questioning at all.

She lay in the sun, naked, her legs apart, luxuriating in the golden light. "I won't go there! I won't live like an ant, or a termite. It would kill me, you; anyone who is really human couldn't stand it." The dream was unrolling backward, Peter thought, interested.

They came for her. Gray men in gray uniforms. Grange was there. He was the director, he had a police bullhorn. "Take her alive. Don't damage her."

"What will you do?" Peter asked Grange.

"Open her head, take out the defective unit, replace it with a factory-fresh component. She'll be better than ever." He winked, "Of course, she'll never play the violin again. Small loss, don't you agree? We can't let anyone with her potential escape, not even temporarily. That was the trouble, you see. We never knew that in the past."

"What about me?" Peter asked.

"We can't use you, you know. Not now. You had your brain blown out in that jungle. Don't you remember?"

"Leave her alone, Grange. Tell them to leave her alone."

They were dragging her to a van. She didn't cry out.

She kept watching Peter all the way. "Tell them to leave her alone, Grange! Tell them!" He didn't want to touch Grange because he knew he would kill him if he did. Grange paid no attention to him and Peter seized him by the throat, squeezed harder and harder. Grange wasn't pretty.

"Peter!" The voice was in the gray city, and in Peter's apartment. He opened his eyes and sat up with a jerk. Lucy was sitting upright on the bed, shivering. "God, what a dream! I haven't had a nightmare for so many years. Hot chilis and guacamole, I guess." He held her, staring at the ceiling until she relaxed again. Deliberately he hadn't asked her to describe her nightmare. If she had wanted to talk about it, he would have tried to stop her. He was shivering, too, and he went to make fresh coffee.

A few minutes later, Peter sat near the bed, drinking coffee.

"Peter," Lucy whispered, "are you there?"

"Sure."

"Peter, I'm not really a convert, you know."

"I know."

She was silent. Surprised that he knew? Then she said, "I thought it would be like religion. You know, you grow up without any. Then you choose one that is okay for you, or least offensive anyway. And you begin to court faith. You participate in everything. All the services. Sing in the choir, if you can, or even if you can't. Work for the fund-raising events. You keep it up, day after day, year after year. Always acting like a convert, hoping one day it'll hit you. The blinding light. Understanding in an instant. Some fucking thing. Only it hasn't yet. It's still all in my head. Still all intellectual." She stopped. Then, "But we have to be able to believe in something. Don't we, Peter? Something, anything, or anyone. Sometimes I feel so afraid because I know there's nothing. We're too small, too few to make a dent in saving the world. Everything just keeps drifting toward whatever it is out there. And I try harder than ever. But I know. I know it's all a Goddamned lie. And I wonder if it is with all the others."

He reached out and caught her hand. And they were silent. He remembered what he had said to D. C. "We have no white whale to chase." And he cursed, but silently, because he didn't want to have to explain to Lucy. And for the first time that day he remembered offering D. C. dinner. After a long time Lucy's hand relaxed in his and finally he put it down gently on the bed.

Chapter 15

Doctor Krump's face was shiny and smooth; his bald dome was shiny, polished. He was a tall heavy man, in his fifties, who looked more like a trucker than a neurosurgeon. His hands were big, with long fingers that played constantly with glasses that Peter never had seen him wear. Prop glasses, he wondered? Had he given up smoking to take up glass playing?

Peter was in a private room this time. Small and nondescript in green and gray, it was all his, with the regulation bed, a high-backed chair, the usual stands, and a bath.

"You'll be comfortable anyway," Krump said, glancing about.

"Why the VIP treatment?"

"It just happened to be available. Why the hell not? Only twenty-four hours." Krump sat in the high-backed chair that creaked under him. Peter sat on the side of the bed. "Tired?"

Peter grinned at him. From nine that morning when he had checked in, they had put him through tests, examinations, paperwork to be filled out, again. Now it was four in the afternoon. They would resume the examinations the following morning. This was the first time that day that he had seen Krump, who would be evaluating results, he knew, and who wasn't needed for the routine.

"Your brother came in to talk to me a week or so ago," Krump said. "He's very concerned about you. Has he mentioned hospitalization?"

"No."

"He described the severity of the attack he witnessed. Is it worse, Peter?"

"Is there a Richter scale for pain?" Peter asked politely. "I described it. The pain wasn't worse, I don't think. But there were differences. I told you about them." He was mildly headachy and afraid that if the headache hit now, they would strap him to the barber's chair, drape him like a tent, and proceed to open the smoke hole to vent his brain. Obviously if he was comatose—what did Krump call it? Carus. Deep coma. If he was, or had? carus, they wouldn't wait for him to wake up to sign a release. Ed would sign in a second anyway.

"He thinks that contrary to your own evaluation there is a gross change in your behavior. He says you are aloof, withdrawn, depressed. That you have long periods of absentmindedness that border on amnesia. That you are sitting on your emotions."

Peter laughed. "Poor old Ed," he said. "I'm not the adoring adolescent, the hero-worshipping kid brother that he thought would come home. You know, we haven't been together much in five or six years. He's over forty, part of the establishment's establishment."

Krump smiled faintly. "All that is irrefutable," he admitted. "Still there is the objective deterioration of your EEG."

"Call it a change," Peter murmured.

"As you wish. But whatever we label it, there is an increase in the epileptiform discharges. There is a new randomness in both beta and theta waves. And there are vertex waves that you never showed before. Your brother's opinion is no more than a subjective judgment that tends to verify these data. The attack you suffered in his house sounds very like an akinetic seizure—severe pain culminating in deep unconsciousness. This is a change that we can deal with, Peter."

He had told them all along that he had abominable headaches, but they had discounted his subjective description of them. Their tests had shown nothing unusual, nothing they didn't expect after surgery like his. Now he had something new, and from Krump's expression, his attitude, it was more or less what he had been waiting for. For the first time Peter had really passed out, not simply gone into a deep sleep, and he assumed the difference was important. And he had had an attack. A fit.

"Epilepsy! Is that your diagnosis of the day?"

"Jacksonian epileptics have symptoms like yours. There are variations in details, but not in essence. We know there is something in the hypothalamus that is stimulating the medial reticular system, making you stay awake. Do you want this?" He waited for Peter's nod, then continued. "Yes. You've been reading about the brain? Right. Your X-rays came out clean, but there are a hell of a lot of things that can go wrong without showing up on the plates. The fact that you sleep after one of those attacks suggests that the reticular system is dysfunctioning, but not destroyed. That's good. Hopeful. All your symptoms derive from a disorder in the thalamus. The pain is unusual as you describe it, but we know very little about pain, what causes it, why acupuncture, for instance, can prevent it. Anyway. Pain isn't adaptive, and if that's good or bad, damned if I know. You don't get used to it. Again, it's the thalamus that maintains and reinforces pain stimuli. You have to notice it and try to relieve it. It precedes, or results in, or is synchronous with stimulation of the substrate of the mass intermedia, again in the thalamus, and finally induces physiologic sleep. We know that stimulation at a point near the lamina medullaris medialis of the right thalamus results in a clonicotonic epileptic fit of Jacksonian type. That's all in the same small area. Jacksonian epilepsy, incidentally, is caused by a trauma of the brain; it isn't genetic."

"So you want to open the little door and have another crack at it." Peter stood up and moved to the window so that Krump wouldn't be able to keep watching him. He felt afraid, and the headache was not quite so mild now. "And next month you might have to do it again. And in two or three more months, again. How many times, Dr. Krump? When does it end?"

There was silence for what seemed too long a time and Peter turned to look at Krump. The shiny doctor was staring at the glasses in his hands. There was a look of great hurt and greater patience on his face. Finally he shrugged and said, "I don't know. I'm consulting with Dr. Marion Raitt in the morning. He's a good man. I had a talk with him about you today, we went over the EEG together. He's a good man," he repeated.

Peter felt a new stiffness in the doctor and studied him thoughtfully.

Krump stood up then and put his glasses in his breast pocket. "I've ordered a mild sedative for you. I know. I know. It probably won't put you to sleep, but you'll rest, I hope."

"Doctor, what do you think is causing the new waves? How bad is it?"

"I just don't know, Peter. I suspect an abscess at the site of a foreign object. A bit of bone fragment, or lining from your helmet."

"Can you get to it?"

Krump started for the door. "I don't know yet. We're talking about the brain stem, and areas deep in the brain tissue. We can't open it up, expose it as we can lungs, or the abdomen, for example. Let's wait for Raitt's diagnosis." He wasn't looking at Peter now; he was plainly anxious to get away from the questioning.

"Dr. Krump, what's wrong? Who is Raitt? Will he be in charge, or will you?"

Krump stopped with his hand on the doorknob. Peter could feel his tension increase as he hesitated. Then he turned and looked at Peter. "Do you trust me, son?" he asked. Peter nodded. "I hope to God you do. Peter, cooperate with Raitt, but don't ask questions. Don't initiate any conversation. Don't anticipate his questions. Raitt's a psychiatrist." Dr. Krump opened the door then and said, "Try to rest, Peter. Maybe the sedative will make you sleep. See you tomorrow."

"Doctor, before you leave, one thing. I've read everything I could find on the brain and its malfunctions. A Jacksonian epileptic, he gets worse, doesn't he? Isn't there a danger of catatonic epilepsy and irreversible coma, or a psychosis?"

"Once it's diagnosed we don't let it go that far," Krump

said. "Tomorrow, Peter. Tomorrow."

Peter was standing at the window as the door closed. He was gripping the sill hard, so hard that his hands hurt. A psychiatrist!

Lil's image of him in a tower with a rifle swam before his eyes. Deliberately he relaxed his hands and began to flex his fingers. She was right all the time, he thought with resentment. Imagine that, the bitch was right all along.

He stayed at the window for a long time. Krump had been trying to warn him about something, but he didn't know what, or why. Krump was on his side, whatever that meant. Krump didn't like, or trust, or perhaps they were the same thing with him? Doctor Raitt. He had the feeling that Krump was no longer in complete charge of his case, but he didn't know why he felt that, or what difference to him it could make. The new tests on the following day were not Krump's tests, and he was to tread carefully, not reveal anything that he didn't have to. Again why?

The questions swirled endlessly, with no answers. At five they brought him food, which was insipid and without substance. At nine he obediently took the capsule that the nurse said was a tranquilizer. At ten they gave him a shot in his hip, and he lay drowsing and half dreaming throughout the night. Twice during the night a young doctor came in to take his blood pressure and pulse. Checking the efficacy of their damned sedative, Peter thought, and submitted without a word.

The next day there was an IQ test, shorter but more difficult than most that he had taken in the past, but he knew he did well on it. There was a thorough eye examination, and then the hearing test, which he stopped arbitrarily at some point that he thought was enough. He could have gone on. Time out for lunch then. After that they did another electroencephalogram. When they started to wire him for a polygraph test, Peter balked, and the technician left to find Dr. Lucas.

"Mr. Roos, do you object? It can cover the same ground that would take dozens of hours of talking with you. Obviously you're not being accused of anything, it is merely diagnostic. We have been having very good results with it as a diagnostic tool."

He didn't give a damn, Peter thought. He was a messenger boy, no more. "No," he said. "I'm not here for analysis. Where's Krump? I want to see Krump."

"Mr. Roos, please be reasonable. We have a very tight schedule. There's simply no time for a consultation in the middle of the testing procedures. You'll have a talk with Dr. Krump at the completion of the various tests he has ordered for you."

"No," Peter said. "Just don't bring that damn thing any closer."

The psychologist shrugged. "I'll call Dr. Raitt," he said, and left.

Peter was in a small office that had the technician's desk with the polygraph apparatus, his chair, and two others, and nothing more. He knew there would be an observation window somewhere, even though it was not apparent. He sat down in one of the chairs and waited. The room was quiet, but not totally soundproofed. Presently he began to hear noises from the adjoining room, a phone being dialed, a low voice, too low to make out the words. He closed his eyes and concentrated on the rhythms of speech that he could hear. An argument. The phone was hung up, and the door that led from the other room to the hallway opened and closed. Presently it opened again and this time there were several voices. He could recognize the technician's nasal tones, and there was Dr. Krump's voice, and a third one that he hadn't heard before. Again he couldn't make out the words—the room was soundproofed enough to prevent that—but he could tell from the interruptions and the rising and falling tones that there was another argument in process. Raitt, he knew. The third voice was Raitt's. He was ordering? asking? pleading with Krump to talk to Peter, to make him agree to the polygraph. Krump didn't want to. Krump's voice got louder and he must have moved close to the door. Peter didn't move a muscle, but he strained to hear.

". . . smacks of entrapment! How could he be a security risk? He's been hospitalized for nearly three years. With amnesia for two of those years."

The other quieter voice cut in, inaudible to Peter. Then Krump said, still near the door, still speaking in a loud voice, "If I can advise him of his rights to refuse to submit, advise him that an investigative branch of the government has requested this test, that it is not for medical purposes. Not otherwise." There was a pause, perhaps the other one was speaking, or lighting a cigarette, or something. Then Krump's voice came again, "He's a sick man, physically sick. He needs the operation now, not lie detector tests and IQ tests. Goddamn it, you know that!"

Someone was dialing the phone again, in the other room. A muted conversation, then the sound of the outer door opening and closing unnecessarily hard. Presently the door opened, and a man entered.

"Peter? I'm Doctor Raitt. How do you do?" His handshake was firm and over with very fast.

Marion Raitt was slender and boyish-looking with sloping shoulders and intense black eyes that seemed interested in everything about Peter, everything in the room. His gaze darted here and there, paused to study the polygraph equipment, then back to Peter, where he paused again. "Look, Peter, I'm afraid that you're not going to like this, but starting next month I'm going to be your doctor here. Doctor Krump is scheduled to go to Germany in March, and well, frankly, we have different methods. He believes in the knife, and I believe in drug therapy. I always say the knife does as much damage, when it's the brain you're talking about, as it undoes. Not a very popular view around a confirmed surgeon like Krump, you'll have to admit."

Peter nodded silently.

"Right. Now, in order to evaluate any drug therapy, we have to have as complete a picture of the patient as we can possibly obtain, and the very quickest method is through scopolamine. The next choice is intensive hypnotic training and questioning, and the next through poly-graphs. Admittedly we can't use the first two. Truth serum has a bad name, frankly. And hypnosis doesn't work as well as some would have you believe. So we're stuck with the lie detector, the same thing that the cops use, or else laborious sessions of questions and answers that can go on as long as ten years, as witness some of the case histories of analyses. We don't have that kind of time, and besides, even if we did, more often than not the patient would be long dead before we were through. You are scheduled for an hour with me later, and I can answer your questions then. What we propose to do now is give you a series of questions, evaluate your responses, and after several weeks on our drug régime do it all over again. This will allow us to judge if the drugs are personality changing, to be avoided, you see, and almost impossible to avoid all the time without such close supervision. I believe fervently that it's better than going through ventriculography again, better than another trip inside your head, especially since the trouble seems to lie in the brain stem. Peter, your chances aren't good for that kind of surgery, not good at all. And it's as simple as that. I'm just sorry that no one filled you in on the details before you were presented with the machinery. I don't blame you for balking."

He smiled easily, the eager boy, anxious to please, to quiet alarms, and under his smile Peter sensed great impatience. Raitt would make a marvelous seducer, sincere, open, fluent, convincing. And Peter was being seduced, with the difference that his body was not the goal, but his brain, what it contained. And he didn't know why. He wondered if he had anything to fear from the test. Wouldn't the questions rather give him an inkling of what they were after? This, too, he knew was part of Raitt's seduction. He knew Peter's capabilities for reasoning, and the clues that had been given to him that there was something unusual about his case. He must have known that Peter would follow such a line of reasoning to this end. Peter felt a growing admiration for the youthful doctor.

Abruptly Peter stood up. "Look, Doctor Raitt, I'm stiff and tired. It's been a strenuous morning. I want to walk a few minutes, stretch my legs, have a drink...at least a cup of coffee."

"Then back here?" Raitt asked smiling. "It won't take long, half an hour at the very most. Then an hour with me. And that'll be it for today."

"Okay. I'll be back up here in half an hour." Peter left the room without looking back. He knew where the canteen was and he walked down the hallway toward the elevators thinking furiously. But it was no use.

The elevator stopped at the second floor and he got off without noticing that it hadn't gone to the basement. Then he realized that it was Krump's floor, that his office was around the corner, and he knew that this was why he had pushed the button after all. Krump was in his office.

"What do they want?" he demanded, before he had closed the door all the way.

"Did you refuse?"

"No. I left for a cup of coffee. I said I'd go back. Who is Raitt, and what does he want from me?"

"He's a neurophysiologist turned psychiatrist. He works for the CIA sometimes, sometimes for the FBI, sometimes for the army. Free-lances, so to speak. He turns up here and there."

"And what does he want from me?"

"Peter, I wish to God I knew. You'd better have that coffee." He buzzed for his nurse, who brought them coffee almost instantly.

"Are you really going to Germany?"

"Yes. It's been scheduled for the end of March for a long time. I had thought I would have your case until then, but I've been taken off. Army, you know." He sipped his coffee, and then put it down. "Peter, you are no longer under jurisdiction of the United States army, you know. As a veteran you can accept VA benefits, or you can forget the whole thing, consult a private physician, place yourself in his hands. I know some good people."

"Dr. Krump, if I signed myself in the hospital today, would you be allowed to operate? If I signed the necessary papers?"

Krump shook his head. "You are Raitt's patient," he said. "He would make the decision."

"By whose orders?" Peter demanded. "Don't I have any say about it?"

Dr. Krump shook his head. "Not in a government hospital. My orders came down through the office of the Surgeon General. There's nothing I can do."

Peter stared at him for a long time. "I'd like the names of a couple of private doctors," he said finally. Get out! Get out! The urge to run was strong, and it was coming from Krump, who would never come out and tell him to run, but would advise him obliquely to get out now. "That private room," he said suddenly. "Raitt meant to try scopolamine on me, didn't he? That's what I was set up for?"

Krump rubbed his eyes.

"And you were so sure that the sedative wouldn't knock me out that you were willing for him to make the effort. You knew there was no risk of its being done without my knowledge." He stopped. "Doctor Krump, this is it, isn't it? This is some kind of political interrogation? I've been accused of something?"

"Peter, see one of these men as soon as you can." Krump wrote several names on his prescription pad. "Tell the receptionist that it's an emergency, that I referred you because of my imminent departure for Germany. I'll get together a file of your medical history today, if I can, and mail it to you to give to the doctor."

Peter's mouth felt dry. "What are the chances, Doctor Krump?"

"I don't know. But they lessen the longer you wait. Better than they were in Japan anyway. A hell of a lot better than when they dragged you out of that jungle and took you to Danang. Just don't delay."

Peter stood up and Krump left his desk to walk to the door with him. "Doctor, thanks. Are you likely to get into any trouble over this?"

"Over what? You decided to have a cup of coffee and as you drank it, you changed your mind about the rest of the tests. That's your right. Good-bye, Peter. Good luck." He shook Peter's hand firmly and opened the door for him.

Peter walked out of the hospital without seeing anyone along the way. Clouds had almost filled the sky, hurrying before the wind that was alive up there, not yet on the surface of the earth. He walked.

Raitt had tried to frighten him into submitting to the lie detector, he thought. And he had frightened him. Ventriculography. They strap you securely, not on a bed, not even on an operating table. Not like anything he had ever been on. Straddling a padded bar. Ride 'em, cowboy! There had been horses once. You're too young, his mother had told him. Wait until you're bigger. He had waited, but never got the horse. They painted his back. Needle? Ah. Local anesthetic. Of course now they'd drill for oil. Or mine gold . . .

There was a needle, too long and too thick. He couldn't see it, but he visualized it anyway, and tensed, waiting for its thrust into his spinal column. He grunted, afraid to try to move now. "Seventeen cc's." They were draining him, pumping out fluid. Then they were replacing it with air. "Let us know when it starts to hurt." Incredible, he thought, awed by the ingenuity of the doctors, a pinprick of a needle and a fire started in his head. There were skyrockets in his visual field, blasts of green that no artist had ever mixed. Green alive with fire. It flared and subsided and flared again.

He could utter no sound. The thing that he was strapped to started to move and the fireworks intensified, brilliant lights that were blinding and faster than he could follow. Nausea rose and pain, deep, deep, where he hadn't realized pain could be felt. They moved him upside down, on his side, on his back, to his stomach, and he retched and made noises that were not human. That was ventriculography. And Raitt had deliberately brought this memory back to him, he knew, walking faster and faster until he was breathless. They would study the plates they made, the air pocket pushed this way and that by a mass of tumor, or abscess, or whatever, and they would know where to look, what to expect when they got there.

This was Krump's tool. This was what Krump and his surgeon friends had to offer. And Raitt? Pills, drug therapy, and the right to peek inside now and then. He was shivering hard.

A garbage can lid skittered past him, and he started and blinked at it. He was soaked to the skin, and the wind was howling about him. It was dark and he didn't know where he was, or how long he had been walking, or what he had been thinking.

He wanted to see Lucy. He wanted desperately to see Lucy then. He hadn't known what time he would get out, and they had agreed that he should pick her up at S.A.F.E. headquarters. He hailed a taxi and gave that address, then sat with his eyes shut tight, willing her to be ready to leave, willing them back in the warm apartment together.

Chapter 16

He rang the bell this time and waited for someone to come. He knew he couldn't face the noise inside. The cold air felt good now, and he wondered if he were feverish, and decided that it was exhaustion that was making his legs feel weak and made the noise from the house seem almost purposely too loud. A girl opened the door finally and Peter blinked at her. She was a child, he thought. What right had they to use children? What could she possibly contribute to anything, except the maturation of a boy equally young, and horny.

"Yes?" she said after a moment.

"Yes. Will you tell Lucy that I'm here. Peter. I'll wait in her car." He said the words carefully, as if speaking to a child who might garble the message.

She smiled, dimpling, and said okay, and the door closed again.

He walked down the street to where he had seen Lucy's car parked, preternaturally aware of his leg muscles as he moved, making a conscious effort to force them to work right, to carry his body the distance. Then he sat down and rested his head on the door frame with his eyes closed. He remained that way until a voice said softly, "Why don't you go elsewhere to wait?"

It was Carl, standing outside the car, leaning forward with his face close to the partially opened window. He was a shadow that seemed to fill the window, and only his teeth gleamed white to relieve the image of a looming blackness ready to overwhelm Peter, swallow him into itself.

"I'll wait here," Peter said.

"She's working," Carl said. Slowly his features were forming from the darkness. Peter could see his eyes now, and his broad nose. He wasn't even a pretty black man, Peter thought. Just typical. Nigger. He didn't know if the word brought the wave of hatred, or if the hatred provided the word, but he sat up. Carl straightened slightly also, and moved back from the door a bit, as if inviting Peter to get out.

"Fuck off," Peter said. "When Lucy tells me she's too busy, I'll go. Not until."

Carl was silent for a moment, and when he spoke again, his voice was flat and hard. "She's got a job to do, and you're getting in her way. We need her."

"You mean you need her. Hire a secretary."

"You don't know her, Roos. You don't know her at all. We need her brain, her training, her knowledge. I won't let her go without a fight."

"Any time," Peter said.

Carl laughed suddenly and his teeth shone. Then he said cheerfully, "You poor simpleminded bastard. Well, I picked up the pieces before, can do it again, I reckon."

Peter pulled the door handle, but Carl held it closed from the outside. "White boy, how you know I don't got a switchblade right here in this hand, just a-waiting to gut you when you step outta that automobile?" He drawled the words, slurring them. Peter felt his face flush and he pushed the door to open it. Again Carl laughed. "Another time, boy. We got plenty of time."

He turned and left, and for a moment Peter watched him. Then he relaxed and let go of the handle of the door. Another time, he said softly. He shivered and closed the window. The car had become very cold.

Carl was a believer in his cause, he realized. He was a messiah, and Lucy was his convert. He wouldn't give her up. His cause was selfless, just, and he was totally dedicated; his very belief would be a bond that was unbreakable. And the cause, Peter wondered. What was the cause? Surely not just to be gadfly to the government. To expose this little scheme here, that one somewhere else, nibbling away at the edges of catastrophe. It's a religion, he thought tiredly, and knew that he was too tired to think it through.

Then Lucy came and he moved over to let her drive, and they went back to his apartment.

In the morning Peter watched Lucy dressing to go back to S.A.F.E. headquarters. She was as unselfconscious as a child. She ate a piece of toast as she hurried into the lacy briefs that she wore. He buttered her another piece of toast. She held it in her mouth and pulled up her flared jeans, then she sat down to drink coffee and juice and milk.

"You look better this morning," she said. "Last night you were ghastly. I'll get off as early as I can, no later than four, and we'll have a quiet evening. Right?"

"Right." They hadn't talked yet. They had both been too tired the night before, and too rushed in the morning. Like old times, Peter thought. Just like old times. Put off the talk until there were hours before them, and then talk and make love and talk some more and eat and make love and talk.... Just like old times. Lucy jumped up and snatched her jersey and pulled it on.

"I have to go, Peter. Today we get out the out-of-town mailings, and then relax for a couple of hours, and start next week's copy. Oh, I almost forgot. I brought a paper for you. This is what went out to the senators and representatives, everyone in town." She had forgotten her hair. He reminded her and she began to brush it.

"Who else gets them?" Peter asked looking over the copy of S.A.F.E. that she had handed him. It was only six pages, but the copy looked dense. There was a very good cartoon by Bruchner. It showed two endless strings of ants, stretching out to infinity; one line, laden with burdens, approached a pit, the other line was of emaciated, empty-handed ants, obviously ready to die now, leaving the pit. One of the ants was saying, "I don't know, something to do with our security."

"Heads of government around the world. All the ecology groups. Governors. Key people in all the state governments. Libraries. All the major newspapers and T.V. news people. Like that." Now she was ready to leave. "Peter, try to rest today. I'll see you as soon as I can." She blew him a kiss on her way out.

Peter washed the dishes and then read the paper. It was ecology-oriented, as he had known. The straight news items were signed, and represented a dozen states at least. The columns and editorials were initialed. He read the lead-in editorial first, Carl's. It was serious and concise and told him nothing he hadn't known. The battle between the opposites: Who is master? Shall the state serve man, or man serve the state? All he learned was that Carl was a good writer. He found another article initialed C. D. This was a dialogue between an angel making a random check on Earth, and a duly appointed spokes-man, elected by the United Nations. It was very funny, satirical, full of puns, sly. So the son of a bitch had a sense of humor, Peter thought bitterly. He looked for Lucy's initials and found them on one rather long column. She could write too. In fact, she might well become a professional writer, he decided, after reading it twice. Her tone was satirical also, and while her humor didn't make him laugh out loud, as Carl's had, it was subtle and good in a wry understated way. Peter finished the paper and decided it was the best of its kind that he had seen. Carl Davis was the senior editor and he did a hell of a job with it, Peter thought, and tried to analyze the mixed feelings that brought. He had hoped, almost, that the paper would be amateurish, maudlin, self-righteous, and instead it was readable, amusing, and to the point. They were working their asses off on it, he thought and felt ashamed suddenly for looking so hard for flaws.

This messiah didn't preach from any pulpit. He didn't stand before the multitudes and perform miracles. But he got his message across, and his congregation was made up of over forty thousand subscribers.

At eleven there was a knock on his door. He opened it to see Ed. He was holding the frame like a mortally wounded man. The skin beneath his eyes looked loose and dirty, a pale green-tinged violet. For an instant, a trick of lighting, or a momentary expression that formed and vanished swiftly, his mother's face seemed to look out at Peter.

"Are you alone?" Ed asked. Peter nodded. "Are you

working for S.A.F.E.?" It was the voice of a stranger.

"Are you going to come in or just stand there and throw questions at me?"

Ed left the doorway and pushed the door shut. It slammed. "Are you a member? On their payroll?"

"What's this all about? What do you mean 'a member'? You make it sound like the Communist Party, or comsymp at the very least."

"And isn't it?"

"No."

"Peter, for the love of God, will you tell me?"

"No. I don't work for them. Now you tell me. What's this all about?"

"That girl, Lucille Shofner. She's the one you lived with in Berkeley, isn't she? Are you living together now?"

"You'd better go, Ed." Peter sat down again at the window.

"Peter, you know I love you. You know that. We've always been closer than just brothers."

Peter watched him. Ed was standing near the door. He looked fifty, a tired, possibly ill fifty. And he looked afraid.

"Do you have anything to drink?" Ed asked. He pulled off his raincoat and tossed it over the couch. Peter started to get up. "Just tell me where. I'll get it."

"In the kitchen, under the sink." Peter followed him to the door and watched him as he found a water glass and half filled it with bourbon. He took his first drink straight, then added water to the remainder and drank again. He looked at Peter then. "You'd better have one too."

"What's going on, Ed?"

"You're linked to the girl. Lived with her over a year before you went in the army. She got into bad company. Arrested on a drug charge. Probation. Suspected of trafficking in drugs after that. Vanished for six months, emerged again as one of the founders and editors of S.A.F.E. A front for anarchy, nihilism, the Panthers. God knows what else. Their methods aren't pretty. Scare tactics. Mass riots. Ban everything. Stir up fear and dissent and suspicion of the government. She was questioned in the California gun case. Again in the New York bomb scares. Not enough evidence to hold her." He drank again.

"Maybe because she hasn't been guilty of anything?" Peter said.

"They'll make it stick this time, Peter. That whole crowd is headed for a conspiracy charge."

"What in hell are you talking about? What conspiracy?"

"Peter, don't look at me like that. Goddamn it, there are conspiracies! And your girl friend is in over her head. And God help us both, you are too."

"A conspiracy to do what?"

"I don't know the formal charges yet. Publishing top secret defense plans. Illegal possession of classified material."

"Balls! Charges that vague never stick."

Ed got up and went to the kitchen to refill his glass. He returned and sat down heavily.

"Do you know what a conspiracy charge would involve? Are you ready for the booking, jail, trial, the whole bit? I couldn't stand for you to go through that. What would it do to Mother? My career? Everything would go down the drain, and you know it. Just check into the hospital, will you? Getting mixed up with all this is a symptom of your illness. I know that, and once you get fixed up again, you'll see it, too."

"If there's a conspiracy I'd damn well have to be part of it by now. As guilty or as innocent as the rest of them. You can't have it any other way. Tell me if you believe there is a conspiracy, Ed. Just tell me that. I want to know.

"I had a call from the hospital," Ed said. His speech was more deliberate. He had almost finished his drink. "Raitt said you should check in, you're risking another attack. He said you could check in tomorrow. Get some rest, lots of rest. Avoid noise and confusion. Might precipitate another attack. Epilepsy. He said it was epilepsy. Did he tell you? Only not the kind that you give your kids, or inherit from your old man. They can treat you, Peter. They can control this kind."

Peter watched him, wondering how much he'd had to drink that morning. He hadn't seen Ed this drunk since a weekend binge he had gone on after Korea.

"What else did Raitt say, Ed?" he asked gently.

"Lots of things. You're in trouble. You ran out before you finished the examinations. You're sicker than you realize, Peter."

Peter felt a chill. That would be the line they'd take. Two consenting physicians, the family's approval. He hadn't foreseen that. That was why he had been transferred from Krump to a psychiatrist. "Ed, do you honestly think I'm mentally deranged?"

"I don't know. How can a layman know anything any more?" Ed's voice was peevish and he didn't look at Peter. "If they didn't think it was important, dangerous even, why would they bother to send someone out to talk to me about you? It's for your own good, Peter. They're concerned about you."

It's for your own good, he thought, and stared at Ed. The chill deepened. Ed was in something much deeper than he had realized, not only the hearings coming up, something more than that. Suddenly he remembered the dream he had had about the city, Ed's admittance to it, his knowledge beforehand that he would be admitted. And he felt that he could almost remember a meeting that had included Ed and Grange and General Ford, and who else? He could remember only those three, although there were other men in the shadows, and behind them, illuminated, a plan of the city. He looked at it with awe; it was too much to take in at a glance. The feeling was one of immensity, a cubic mile of city, layers separated from layers by the rock of the earth itself. There were five major sections, each devoted to a different phase of activity. Each section was a thousand feet high, subdivided into floors, some ten feet high, others rising fifty feet, one hundred feet. On the lowest levels would be the atomic energy plants, the military, the weaponry development areas, training grounds.

On other levels were areas designated R and D, Hydroponics, Animal Research, Living Areas, Recreation, Industrial, Administration.

Peter realized that he had been thinking in terms of stress and load-bearing capacity, subjects about which he knew nothing. It would be safe, he thought. What they removed had greater mass than what they put back in, much greater specific weight. Safe, he thought again, with longing. Abruptly the images and words vanished. Peter felt the warmth of the room return.

Ed had stood up and was on his way to the bathroom, his face very white. Peter heard him being sick, and in a few minutes he returned, still pale, but less visibly drunk.

"Can't remember when I've had a drink before lunch," he said. "You have coffee made?"

Peter made coffee and Ed washed his face and combed his hair and smoked while he waited for it. They sat across from one another at the small table and Peter said, "Ed, you're in trouble, aren't you? Over me?"

"I don't know," Ed said slowly. "It has been suggested that I leaked material to you that you then passed on to your friends at S.A.F.E. You know that's not so, but . . . Yes. It could mean trouble."

"And if you talk me into going back to the hospital, signing myself in, that would get you off the hook?"

Hope lightened Ed's face and he nodded without speaking.

"But, Ed, what could you have leaked to me that would matter to anyone?"

"I don't know. Believe me, Peter, I honestly don't know. Unless they sincerely suspect that you are an agent of some sort. But I haven't leaked anything to you, ever. You haven't been to the office. There's been no way. Still . . ."

"It's a frame," Peter said, still speaking softly. "You know, and I know, and they know that I'm not an agent." He didn't push it further. Ed didn't know why they wanted him. "Do you know who Raitt is?" he asked.

Ed flushed dully. "Will you sign yourself in? Let them treat you?"

"No. I decided to stop taking advantage of the government's generosity. I decided to consult a private doctor and let him handle everything for me."

"You couldn't afford it! Do you have any idea what it would cost you?"

"You have any idea of how much money I managed to save out of my pay while I was snoozing away in that Goddamn hospital?"

"Peter, don't do this. Please."

"Tell Raitt he won't see me again, Ed. I'm through with all of them. If they want me they'll have to trump up a charge and arrest me, and they'd better have enough to make it stick."

"It wouldn't be like that," Ed said dully. He was staring at his coffee cup, avoiding Peter's gaze. He lifted the cup and his hand was shaking.

"It would be the white-coated men, wouldn't it, Ed? With a legal certification, okayed by you, or Dad maybe, duly signed by a couple of doctors. You'd rather see me back in the hospital, a certified head case, than have me drag all of us through a conspiracy charge. It would save me, wouldn't it? Less damaging to me than the arrest because I have a legitimate cause of psychological trouble. A year, two more years, then out again, cured."

"Don't do that!" Ed said, trying to put his cup down on the table again, his hand shaking too hard now to keep control. The cup fell to the floor and smashed, spewing coffee in all directions.

"Don't do what, Ed?"

"Peter, you're sick! My God, do you think I'd even consider such a thing if I didn't know you were sick? They said you could become dangerous, to yourself or others."

Peter continued to watch him, and Ed stook up shakily. He stared at the bits of cup on the floor, and looked as if he was going to weep. "Time, that's what we need now. Nothing too soon. They're pressing me too hard. You're pushing. Everyone's always pushing. I have to clean up that mess, don't I?"

"Ed, just don't do anything for a while. Will you promise me that much? Let me see a private doctor first. I'll keep in touch about how it goes. Don't let them push you too far too fast, Ed."

Ed weaved back and forth. He looked as if he might be sick again. "There isn't any time," he said. "Today, tomorrow. You have to be in the hospital by tomorrow. Peter, if you love me, if you've ever loved me, please do this thing." He was going to weep, Peter thought. Ed was staring at him, his face stricken, ashen. "We've always looked out for each other, Peter. You scared me, you always caught on so fast to everything I showed you. Everything. One time and you had it. I used to wonder if there was a limit to what you could learn. I watched you in school, gobbling up everything they tossed at you. You never knew how I had to struggle, hit the books all night, night after night, just to get by. And you breezed through it all. I used to tell people about you, my little brother, the genius. Proud. I was proud of you all the time. When you were in the hospital, I wouldn't go see you. Not until you were yourself again. You realize that? Mom and Dad could go look at you, tubes up your nose, in your arms, everywhere. I never could. I cried like a baby when they told us about you. If there had been any way on God's earth to change places with you then, I would have done it, Peter. I really would have done it."

"I know, Ed." Peter thought of his deals with God when Ed had been in Korea. He said again, "I know."

"Let me help you now, Peter. I couldn't before. But now I can. Please let me."

"Ed, do you realize what Raitt intends to do? Do you understand modern, medical interrogations?"

"They wouldn't hurt you. And you have nothing to fear from them. You've done nothing!"

"Then why should I have to submit to it?"

Ed turned away from him and fumbled with his chair, trying to straighten it so he could sit down again. "They wouldn't hurt you," he said, sulkily. "Then Krump, or someone like Krump, would be called back in."

The door was flung open suddenly and D. C. ran in. "Senator, are you all right? Mrs. Roos has been trying to find you."

"D. C.! Good, trustworthy D. C. How many men are fortunate enough to have an aide like her, Peter? Smart, pretty, loyal."

"Peter, what have you been pouring down him? Come on, Senator. Let's go get some coffee. You can't go home like this."

"You want some help?" Peter asked, as Ed walked toward her unsteadily. "I don't think he's eaten anything today. Never used to hit him like that."

Ed put his hand on D. C.'s shoulder. "Is it far? Where you are taking me."

She looked at Peter; her cheeks flushed a deep pink, then paled. She put her arm around Ed. "Not far," she said, and her voice sounded very distant and muffled.

Peter watched them navigate slowly and carefully down the hall. And when he went back inside his apartment, he opened all the windows as wide as they would go and let in the cold, bad city air, because no matter how foul it was, it seemed better to him than the odor that lingered in the rooms. And then he began to clean up the smashed cup and wipe the coffee stains off the floor, off the table legs. He told himself that the burning behind his eyes was due to the polluted air that was whistling through the room.

Chapter 17

At two-thirty Peter had a call from Grange.

"Look, Peter. I'm all alone for once. Why don't you drop in for a drink, some talk."

"Now?"

"Yes. I have to go out at four, so now. Okay?"

"Sure," Peter said. He hung up slowly. Ed had had time to report failure, and now Grange would try, he thought bleakly. He wrote a note for Lucy, just in case she got there early, and went out. It was gray, misty, not very cold, typical pre-spring weather. Grange admitted him to the suite and took his coat, tossed it carelessly to a chair and led Peter into the living room where a table was set up for drinks.

"Scotch and water? I thought I remembered that." He mixed the drinks and motioned Peter to a chair. "I've been thinking a lot about you, Peter. I want you back." He raised his glass in a salute and then drank. "You were the best damn student I've had in fifteen years."

Peter tasted his drink. "I would have thought Lucy was the best," he said.

"Ah, Lucy, lovely, little, pixyish Lucy with the flighty brain." Grange laughed easily and drank again. "You know she left soon after you did? Hell, I wrote and asked you for her address. Remember? There was some trouble with acid. She got spooked and ran. She wasn't threatened with arrest, nothing really serious, I understand." He clinked his ice, then made it go round and round. He watched it interestedly. "It was too bad. But then, I've seen it before. Brilliant women students who suddenly seem to realize where they are, what they're doing, what the competition is. It doesn't matter a damn that they can hold their own. They run like hell. You begin to resent the time wasted on them. Then another one comes along, with an IQ high enough to make you blink, and you do it again. I was bitterly disappointed when Lucy ran." They both had become wary. Peter was too still, Grange too alert, watchful. Peter tried to relax, and took another small sip of his drink. Grange went on. "Funny thing about women. So damned afraid of success. Something left out of them I suppose. Or cultural conditioning, more likely. A damn shame."

He stood up abruptly and reached for Peter's glass, then frowned at him because it was still nearly full. He made another drink for himself, talking, his back to Peter now. "However, back to you. What are you doing? Have you made plans at all?"

"Not yet. I haven't actually been discharged from the hospital. I'm an outpatient. I was staying with Ed, my brother, you know. Senator Roos. Doing a little reading for him. Summarizing scientific articles relevant to the DEDF project."

"The most exciting proposal I've ever worked on!" Grange sat down, his back to the windows, and leaned toward Peter.

"Why? It's not even new. Just technologically more possible now. What's exciting about it?"

"It would mean the creation of a total environment, not random this time, but planned in every detail. Perhaps it's the only way to save civilization. Put the polluting industries under the surface of the earth; the earth above will revert to Eden. Inexhaustible energy from fusion for all the centuries to come."

"We don't even have a fusion process yet."

"Not today, but soon. Ten years from now, fifteen. We'd have to start with fission, true, but with fusion a certainty in the very near future." He waved Peter's objection aside. "It would be safe, no matter which we used. The reactors in the lowest level, separated from any living thing by five hundred feet of concrete, rocks, earth. Over a mile deep, its waste products much deeper than that even. Let them scream of radioactive contamination. We'll show them our geologists' reports. The thermal energy of the earth is created by nuclear reactions. We'd be peeing in an ocean."

"There's some pretty stiff opposition. And some good people. They can come up with a case for the other side."

"Horseshit. When it's steam engine time, it's going to appear. It's deep earth defense facilities time. Listen, are you going to come back and pick up where you left off? Or not exactly there. But somewhere?"

"Why not finish my work on the duplicating inhibitor?"

"It's a blind alley. After you left I went over everything and Wesselman and I followed through on your notes for the next three months. I can't bring all the details to mind. Wesselman did most of the work, and I reviewed it. I'll give you our findings, his notebooks, the works. Good negative data. We published, of course. Give it all to you as soon as I get back to Berkeley."

We published, of course, Peter thought. Of course. He wondered if Grange had published anything in the past five or six years that hadn't been graduate student work, published under the joint authorship of teacher and student. Okay, he thought, more quietly, you expect that, accept it as a fact of life. But you don't accept a toad like Wesselman signing his name to your half. "You had no right to let Wesselman have my work," he said tightly.

"No right? You had no rights!" Grange jumped up, his voice higher, his words fast now. "That was my experiment. My line of thought. I needed that proof. I needed to prove that differentiation occurs when specific requirements are met, chemical chains that the mass of cells themselves generate spontaneously." His face was dark, but no expression was there, only his high-pitched voice betrayed his excitement. "To prove what I knew had to be, I had to disprove a lot of nonsense first. You think I would have waited for you to come back? Not even if you had gone to the corner drugstore, Peter, not even then."

He began to pace swiftly about the room. "You were dead. They told me that you'd died, that you'd never recover. That if you did live, you'd be a vegetable. Rights! I had to know. Listen, Peter, let me tell you something. I

know what they say about me. Money grabber. I am. I
need money, and no one ever left me any. My old man
clerked in a hardware store! Fame grabber. Sure. It's
great fun to be famous, make people bow, make
presidents and prime ministers plan visits at your
convenience. But none of that means a shit compared to
the moment when something big has worked out. The
moment you know that you have a piece of the universe,
that no one on earth but you knows this truth, that
everyone, *everyone* will be affected by what you alone
know. That's as near as man can come to being God!
That's the only transcendental experience! That's what
the goal is, everything we do to get there is incidental. If
you could get there stirring shit in a pan, you'd stir shit for
the rest of your life. Twice I've had it, Peter. Twice I've
had a piece of the universe in my hands. And if I thought I
could have it again, but for you, or anyone else alive, I'd
kill you to get you out of my way."

Peter had forgotten what a passionate man he was.
Lucy said he was incapable of passion with a woman. The
sexual act with him would be quick, functional, a need to
be satisfied as effectively and effortlessly as possible. "But
he is always seen with beautiful women," Peter had
pointed out. "His position demands that much," she said.
"Grange has to have a house like no one else has, on a hill
with a view, all that crap. Impeccable clothes. Beautiful
woman at all times. You haven't contradicted anything I
said before. His vanity equals his intelligence, that's all."

Grange was still flushed. He put down his glass and lit a
cigarette. Obviously for something to do; he smoked very
little. "Well," he said, blowing smoke. "You touched a
nerve. It's that word: rights. Too much trouble at school.
Too many bombs and bomb threats. Too many personal
threats. And all the time prattling on and on about
rights." He laughed suddenly. "It's really those interminable speeches that get to me. My God, those awful, awful
serious speeches."

"You listen to them?"

"Nobody listens to them, not really. They come in by
osmosis. Let's not talk about them anymore. God, I'm

tired of them all. All sound and fury, four-year-olds' foot-stamping, demanding this and that." He laughed quickly, a nervous humorless laugh. "I know how fashionable it is these days to damn technology, and my God, I agree. The billions going into weaponry! My God! But that's blind technology—doing what we can do only because we can do it, have the tools, the machinery, the engineers to do it. And the military has cornered the scare market. But if you harness that same technology to a dream, Peter, yes, call it utopia, if you will." Grange was very close to Peter, the laughter gone, his voice low and urgent. "And, Peter, we need the dreamers who are also skilled, trained, educated. Can a bricklayer advise a surgeon? Can a shopkeeper vote on subatomic physics? We need the highly trained dreamers, Peter. People like you. For the first time in the history of civilization there will be a real need to establish a meritocracy. And, Peter," he said, even more intently, "do you have any idea of where these very good people will go if we don't get our facilities, guaranteed facilities, without the usual year-to-year renewal of funds? They'll go back to high-school teaching, if they're lucky. They'll go to work in the factories, or doing cleanup work after the factories. There's no money these days, Peter. And there will be even less in the days ahead. There are no more NSF funds. No more big grants, no more private philanthropic grants. I've been cut back forty percent, Peter. Me! Can you imagine what it's been like for others?"

"Why? The whole world's waiting for the magic cures for everything."

"They're waiting. But they expect us to produce the magic sitting in armchairs scribbling in a dime store notebook. Three times in the past two years it has been proposed that a commission be set up to determine in which area research scientists should be allowed to pursue their studies. Three times!"

"Who would make up such a commission?" Peter asked.

"Bricklayers! What Goddamn difference would it make who was on it?" He swung around and said, very quietly, very firmly, "We're in real trouble, the whole world is. You think those pork barrel politicians can come up with answers? Goddamn it, Peter, they don't even know enough to ask questions. Those who can understand have to move now. Even now might be too late. Yesterday might have been too late. One of those asses is going to start something that will blow it all apart, something that no one can stop, and when it blows, we'll be there in the ashes, you, me, all of us smoldering in the same ashes." He took a deep breath and, eyeing Peter steadily, deadly serious, he said, "I think you're one of us, Peter. Four years ago you weren't, but you have matured. They are phasing out science from the federal budget and only the federal government has the kind of money to finance it."

His voice became almost light, bantering, "I know more about the Goddamned cellular processes than any man alive today, and they would have a plumber tell me what to do next. That's what's in the air today, Peter, my boy. That's the brave new world we're coming to."

Peter shook his head. "It all got too fat. Too many Ph.D.'s, too many academic chairs, too much of everything. It'll level out again."

"No," Grange said bitterly. "Not this time. It can all stop, you see. Not because they're afraid of what we might do, although God knows they are and maybe they should be. It'll stop because we're catching up with the easy things, and the hard things simply cost too damned much. More and more elaborate equipment every year. The questions get harder, and the solutions more costly. That's what will bring it to a stop. Those plumbers and bricklayers will think of what they could do with this three million dollar grant, or that two million, and we'll never see it." Grange finished his drink and put the glass down. "Think of the things that can be accomplished within this decade. You know them as well as I do. Cancer cures. An end to hereditary defects. A general increase of intelligence of everyone, right down the line. Even more important things that we simply can't predict."

Peter felt that he must be registering disbelief, for suddenly Grange laughed. "Sure, I'm selfish. I want to continue my work, but in this one instance my own selfishness pays off to humanity. And they're stopping me, Peter. They're stopping me. I need more assistants, more equipment, more freedom. And what do I get? A forty percent cutback!"

Peter stood up. "I just can't believe it's all that simple. The city plan wouldn't solve anything. Economically it would be disastrous. I read about the Harbor Study, done back in the fifties. Simple tunnels under the cities of a quarter million population or more, that's all it amounted to. And the cost then would have been thirty-nine billion dollars! But this scheme! One of the city levels would cost that much more. The gains and the cost are too disproportionate. It's the dream of an economic idiot."

Peter wasn't certain why he wanted to goad Grange suddenly, unless to force him to reveal more, to reveal something pertinent. He felt frustrated not knowing even now why he had been called, why Grange had invited him to have this talk. Certainly not because he wanted him back. Grange wasn't even pretending to pursue that.

Grange laughed. "Money. Do you know what the carnage on the highways costs each year? Or the obsolescence of senseless military equipment? Don't make like a financial expert unless you have some figures, Peter, my boy. The role doesn't suit you." He stood up and went to the window, where he stood with his back to Peter. "Come to the hearings, Peter. Maybe you'll change your mind. Now, if you'll excuse me."

The abruptness of his dismissal startled Peter. He nodded and went to the door and pulled on his coat. Grange followed him, made no motion toward helping him with his coat, or to shake his hand. Peter felt awkward momentarily, then simply left without saying good-bye. As Peter walked toward the elevator, he heard the door close softly. Something, something, he thought. He stopped, and suddenly he visualized a yellow lined pad, and a sketch of a city on the pad. The sketch he had made in Ed's study one night. Without volition his body turned and he was walking slowly back, watching the carpet before him.

". . . we all know he's an ass. Nothing surprising there. So he blabbed about the city plans and Peter picked it up. That's all there is to it." Grange was looking at the sketch Peter had drawn, Peter knew. He could almost feel the way the paper crinkled in Grange's hand, he could see the light reflected on a third of it, his erasure marks, dark smudges here and there. "Look, Ford, I don't give a damn what you do with him. Hand him over to Raitt and forget him. You can't blame his brother for trying to protect him. But there's nothing he can tell. Peter can't know more than the Senator does, and that's damn little. So relax." Another silence, and during it, Peter could feel Grange's impatience and scorn. Finally Grange cut in. "Goddamn it, Ford, I know this boy. If he had anything, I would know it. All he knows is that there are plans for a city. That's a lot of bullshit!" He subsided and said, in his most reasonable voice, "I tell you he can't hurt us, or help us. No way." And there was an image of a map and a city that seemed to blur together then separate, then merge again. "Roos doesn't even know where it is, Ford. For God's sake!"

Peter leaned against the wall in the corridor, feeling a numbness in his legs and hands, almost as if he were slipping into shock. Again the city firmed, and it was like one of his many newly revived memories, incomplete at first, but with more and more details coming into focus steadily. Not his memory, he thought distantly, not his memory at all. Still details formed and became clear. There was a deep excavation, a mountain of earth surrounding it, and many trucks, tractors, machinery that he didn't understand. Construction men in hard hats, military guards everywhere. And mud and snow and frozen ground away from the deep hole. The snow was black. Peter could no longer feel his arms and legs, the numbness was spreading to his hips and his shoulders. He felt farther and farther removed from the man leaning against the wall, and viewed him with some sympathy and some regret. He really should move, he thought. He should push himself away from that wall and move to the stairs and start walking down them, right now. He should not wait for the elevator. He wondered, with interest, if the numbness would affect the action of his lungs, his heart. Grange slammed down the telephone and threw an ashtray across the room. For now, he was thinking. For now. But wait! Six months, a year. Just wait, Ford, and Roos, and Marko. All of you!

He really should move, Peter thought, but it wasn't Grange alone. A woman terrified about a lost earring. A man cursing monotonously under his breath visualizing another man dead in one grotesque scene after another. A youngster heady with marijuana, fantasizing. More and more of them. Now Grange was yanking on an overcoat, and halfway down the hall Peter was slumped against the wall, staring at nothing. The distant Peter came back. *Move! Move!* And somehow Peter was lurching away from the wall, toward the red Exit sign. He moved woodenly, drunkenly, rolling into the wall, bouncing off it again. He pulled the door open and felt a blast of cold air from the stairwell, and it seemed that somewhere else a door closed and silence returned. Weakly he sat down on the top step and put his face in his hands.

He walked finally, looking at nothing that wasn't in the line of vision directly in front of him, two square yards ahead of his feet. On both sides buildings shimmied, advanced and retreated; people on the sidewalks were blurred moving lumps that glowed, dimmed, glowed. He was hallucinating, he thought. Hallucinations, both audio and visual now. Phase three? He remembered one of the doctors—Dr. Seligman?—who had said, "You may find that you will have periods of what can only be called waking dreams, periods of mental activity not unlike REM sleep. Keep a record of them for us, will you?" But the experience he had had was not like a dream, he knew. It wasn't going away, dimming at the edges, merging with consciousness. The image of the map was stronger than it had been when he had first visualized it. Stronger and more insistent. And the rest of it. He remembered how the yellow paper had felt, how it had rustled.

His legs began to throb sometime later and he realized that he had been walking so fast that he was breathless; he didn't know how long he had kept up this pace. He looked about trying to orient himself, but he was in a part of the city that was unfamiliar. He went into a drugstore and ordered coffee and then began to dissect his experience in the hall. He had hallucinated. He had imagined the voices and fears of people in the building and for a time they had been very real to him. He tried to explain the map he had seen, and the sketch, and he found that he was unable to think about either of them in any objective way. Finally he gave it up and left the drugstore and found a cab stand.

And he knew that something had happened that was frightening, too frightening to think about.

Chapter 18

D. C. had been waiting for him. When he passed her door, she came out and walked to his apartment with him.

"Who is the girl?" she asked, following him inside his apartment. She was wearing a thigh-length red shirt over flowered bell-bottoms.

"An old school pal."

She sat on the couch, and took out a cigarette. "Is she still around? Or just a one-night stand? With a rerun now and then thrown in?"

"Don't be vulgar."

"Heaven forbid." She examined her cigarette filter carefully, then tapped it a time or two, concentrating on it. "She's pretty. Hippie?"

"Why do you ask?"

"I shouldn't, should I? I mean it's self-evident. Blue jeans, long hair, the decal on her car window."

"I don't mean that," Peter said patiently. "I know you're clever. You didn't have to ask. Why do you care?"

"And again, I shouldn't, should I? Our agreement back in the beginning. No strings. No obligations. Maybe I really don't care, just generally bitchy." She lit the cigarette, then stubbed it out too violently. "That girl. She's trouble, for you, for Ed, for everyone. She's mixed up with whatever Carl Davis is planning, and as long as she's mixed up with you too, that makes for an interesting *ménage à trois*, doesn't it. You can't be left out if she's in. Not if you're playing house with her. This isn't a kids' game, Peter." She got up and went to the door, where she stood looking at him for what seemed to be a long time.

"All my life," Peter said, "They kept telling me, 'Think how it would look. Consider your brother, his position.'"

"That's the only important thing there is to consider,"

she said flatly. "And if it kills your little ego to admit it, open your eyes and see if there's anything else worth a damn."

"What happened with Ed this afternoon?" Peter asked suddenly. "Was he too drunk to lay?"

"You can be filthy, can't you?"

"You bet I can. Ed's in something so rotten you can smell the stench for miles. Do you know what it is, D. C.? Do you care? Or is it my man—right or wrong? They think they have it covered over, but it won't stay covered. But you're all too busy playing games, aren't you? And your side has all the money, and the jails, and the power to fill them. You'll have to fill them. And then build more. You're all crazy! All of you. You're a bunch of Goddamn lunatics!"

"If I had your head I'd be awfully careful about who I called crazy," she said coldly. "You're not just naïve. You're stupid. And around here that's the only unforgivable sin."

"What did you come here for, D. C.? Not to exchange insults with me?"

"I came because I had a romantic schoolgirl notion that I owed you something. And I pay my debts. The Justice Department is ready to move against them. They have been receiving classified material, and there's to be an injunction to prevent their publishing it. And they'll stand tried for conspiracy to obtain and publish classified material. Peter, so help me God, if you've been feeding them anything from your brother, if you involve him, I'll see you in hell for it." She opened the door and then said, "And, Peter, if you try to get yourself admitted to a private physician's care, they'll serve you with a certification, all duly signed and authorized and everything. Check into the hospital, Peter. Let Raitt take care of you."

He stared at her, trying to see past the smooth face, set in a look of dislike now, but there was nothing to see, nothing to feel from her. She emitted nothing. "Paid in full?" he asked finally.

"Paid in full." She left, closing the door softly.

Peter sat down. It was almost six. He felt as if the day had been going on for weeks. And the thought of the hospital and Raitt and Krump hovered always now at the edge of awareness so that when he let go, it came back in with a rush and he saw the long needle and the padded chair. He sat down and watched the lights of the city in the murky darkness.

He wished that Lucy would hurry. He would grill the steaks, toss the salad, pour the wine. They would make love and talk and make love again, and sip more wine, and presently she would sleep and he would be able to relax then.

He closed his eyes; the headache that had started in the hospital was still with him. Like fear, it was always there ready to claim his attention if he let it. After a few minutes, he opened his eyes and the room was a blur about him, a melting of colors and edges into other colors, other edges. He rubbed his eyes and the colors and edges firmed up and stopped weaving except at the periphery of his vision. He knew that he didn't care to try to examine what was happening to his peripheral vision. The ophthalmologist had said, "Hm," over it, nothing more.

He made coffee then, and got out his atlas. An eastern state, he thought. The vision he had had outside Grange's apartment was fresh in his memory, but he had made out no names on it, and he wasn't sure about his reasons for thinking it had been in the east. He hoped alternatively that he would find it, and that he would not. Maine. Nothing. Massachusetts. Nothing. Connecticut. Nothing. He found the location in upper New York State, in Erie County. He stared at the map for a long time. It was the site of a proposed atomic power plant, not yet begun four years ago when the map had been copyrighted. Isolated, inaccessible, a valley surrounded by steep hills. He pushed the atlas away, leaving it open, and started to sketch the city that he had seen. His movements were almost mechanical. He wasn't trying to remember anything, merely sketching without thought those images of the city that he seemed to possess.

When he finished he had six sketches, different views

of the same city. The first was the largest, a freehand copy of the architectural drawing. The rest were fragments, the images an architect might visualize from an abstract blueprint. The moving sidewalk and the background of windowless façades, the people in gray, expressionless; the elevator that had no inside controls; an avenue that apparently was meant to represent a regular city street, windows in the buildings, a pseudo-sky overhead with paste-up clouds; the checkpoint manned by a gray-clad attendant, with armed guards... Abruptly he turned the sketches over and stared dully ahead.

Ed's dream. Ed had seen those plans, had known he was one of the chosen. He must think that this city represented good for many people, that it was even necessary; his betrayal was of an abstract principle, his oath of office, the trust of his constituents, his colleagues. Peter's betrayal was personal, a brother betraying a brother. Ed had accused Peter and his contemporaries of being cynical once, and yet it was he who had taken the cynical course. Expecting nothing except chaos in the future, he was trying to insure against that chaos with his underground city to preserve the few, abandoning the many to the disruption he foresaw: war, pollution crises, whatever evil it was he feared. And his act of abandonment would become one of the causes of the crisis he feared.

When Lucy came in, Peter had his sketches and his map in a folder. He kissed her. "Let's take a walk."

"Peter! Why? I'm beat, and there's something that I have to tell you." She looked exhausted and she was radiating gloom.

"You can tell me while we walk. I forgot the wine for dinner. Come on."

She looked at him sharply, then cast an involuntary glance about the room. He nodded, and she seemed to slump even more. "Great. I get to pick it this time. You've been feeding me Kool-Aid or something with a touch of sulphuric acid."

The wind was hard, and there were few people on the streets. The air smelled acrid and old. Tired air, Peter thought. "You first," he said, holding her arm tightly.

"We got a call about you today. The caller said you were a plant. There was a lot of discussion about it and about half our people think we shouldn't see each other for awhile, until after this hassle with the hearings, anyway. Carl made them stop pressuring me, but suddenly everything has become grim, nasty. We've never been suspicious of each other before."

Peter made a snorting sound and put his arm about her shoulders. "I'm only surprised they didn't do it before." They passed a small restaurant with booths and not many people and he steered her inside. Quickly Peter told her about Ed's visit, and D. C.'s warning. She rearranged her napkin, water glass and silverware studiously while he talked about D. C.

"We knew we had a plant," she said finally. She avoided looking at Peter. "And I guess it's never a surprise anymore to know you might be arrested at any moment. It's the unfairness of it that hurts." She sounded like a little girl being beaten in a game whose rules she didn't understand. A waiter came and they ordered ham sandwiches and coffee. Lucy kept playing with her knife and fork. "Why are they so hot this time, Peter? Why this kind of pressure?"

He still held the folder. With his other hand he reached across the table and covered her restless hands. She looked up at him. "You walked into something a lot more crooked than you could imagine," he said soberly. "Much worse than you think it could be."

She stared at him and said, "Your brother will be in the middle of it, when it blows, then."

He said nothing.

"They don't intend to let anything break, do they? That's why the arrest threats, the injunction. They intend to keep it all under wraps one way or another." She became silent, watching him, then finally said, "There's something else, isn't there?"

Not yet, Peter thought, not yet. He asked, "Have you done anything with your music?"

The waiter came with their sandwiches. Peter let her

hands go and sat back. She picked up her sandwich, put it
down again. "Nothing. It wasn't relevant." There was a
mocking note in her voice, self-mockery. "No Chopin this
year. I've tried to play and couldn't. It came out ugly. No
matter what I wanted to play it came out a dirge."

"Yeah," Peter said moodily. He reached for her hand
and held it too tightly. He loosened the pressure when she
winced. "They're out to get you, honey. They'll arrest you,
make you stand trial on a bummer, that they know is a
bummer. You've got a plant, maybe a dozen plants.
They've probably fed you classified material. God only
knows what they'll come up with. And, Lucy, what for?
What good are you doing? No one's watching anymore.
They got bored and turned you off."

"I know," she said sadly. "We're playing our hearts out
and it's an empty theater. Dinosaur time is running out,
but they won't hear you saying that. *They* realized
suddenly that our scenario was real, that our third act
shows them all dead or dying. They left in droves then.
They're all home watching reruns of *The Beverly
Hillbillies.* No one wants to know any more."

He kept thinking of her music and he knew this was the
worst part of it all. Death of music, beauty. If it wasn't
relevant, the world had no use for it.

"You know that if you get arrested they might hold you
until the trial, don't you?" She nodded. "They'll certainly
hold Carl. Could you take that? You. Carl."

"I don't know." She pushed her sandwich away. "It
isn't just Carl and me. There are others. Mary, Spivak.
My God, we have seven editors!"

"How did you get into the newspaper business
anyway?"

"Oh, it just happened. Carl had started it before I met
him. But he had a mimeo sheet and a couple of hundred
subscribers then. You remember that I took some writing
courses and a journalism course as electives a thousand
years ago? I was out of school, out of a job, out of luck,
and he began talking about reorganizing the paper, and
we got together with a few others and S.A.F.E. came out
of the whole thing. We have forty thousand subscribers

now. We're doing a good job, Peter, a worthwhile job."
Again the hurt was there.

"And now you're homing in on something too hot to
touch," he said, and he moved his hand from the folder.

She nodded solemnly. "We thought the SST thing was
a hot potato, but it wasn't anything like this. We've been
bugged from Day One of our stay here. Carl is being
followed. Maybe I am, but I'm not clever enough to spot
him." She leaned forward, closer to him, and said in a
whisper, "And, Peter, we don't even know why. We don't
even know what it is that we're supposed to have. What it
is they're afraid we have."

Abruptly Peter stood up and tossed a five-dollar bill on
the table. "Let's walk," he said.

On the sidewalk again Lucy turned to look at him.
"What is it, Peter? What's wrong? Was it your hospital
report?"

"I have to talk to you and Carl," he said. "In private.
Can he arrange it?"

She nodded. "Now?"

"Now."

He waited while Lucy made the phone call in a
drugstore, and they walked again, slowly, waiting for Carl
to come along and pick them up. Lucy was silent, but
from time to time she looked up at him—fearfully,
wistfully? He couldn't decipher her glances. Peter
imagined every person they passed was an agent of some
sort, watching, listening, using ultramodern devices that
could not only pick up their every whisper, but their every
thought as well. When Carl pulled to the curb and they
got in, Peter wondered if the old Dodge was bugged.

"Let's take the bus," Carl said. He parked the car in a
lot, and they walked to the corner and waited. It was very
cold. No one else was at the stop. The bus, when it came,
was nearly empty.

"Now?" Peter said, seated in the rear of the bus, Lucy
at his side, Carl in the side seat half facing them. He
nodded.

Peter told him quickly about the pending injunction,
the arrests to come. "They're building a prototype city,"

Peter said, keeping his voice low. "I have sketches of what it will be like when it's done. Not just a defense installation, an entire city. And I have a map with the location. Can you use any of this?"

Carl was regarding him with his blank expression, his eyes flat, almost without reflection, as if all his light was being kept hidden purposely. Slowly he nodded. "All classified, stolen? From your brother?"

"He doesn't know anything about it. He knows about the plans for an eventual city, but he doesn't know it's being built right now."

Carl didn't believe him. Lucy averted her gaze.

"I know he's in it," Peter said wearily. "Up to his ears, but he doesn't know how far it's gone." He hesitated, then shrugged. "I can't tell you how I got it." He wondered what they would say if he told them the truth. I don't know how I got it. He made a motion to extend the folder toward Carl, an easily overlooked motion, if Carl decided to overlook it.

Carl didn't move yet. Softly, smiling gently, he said, "You remember that day you came knocking, looking for Lucy? Ralph nudged me and I turned and saw you standing there, and I thought, 'Yes, by God, this is the break!' That's what I thought, Peter. Then you asked for Lucy, and it went away fast, boy, real fast. I forgot it, in fact. Fact. I forgot it. I'm not like them poor southern field blacks who believe in premonitions and hunches and spells. Not me. Too civilized, too educated for that kind of nonsense. But funny things happen. It came back. When we exchanged pleasantries out by the car. I remembered it all at once, out of nowhere. And I thought, yeah, but, he's poison for Lucy and you know it, and I shushed that other voice awfully fast. And when they wanted to vote on keeping you away from S.A.F.E., I remembered it again, and I wouldn't let them do it. Funny, don't you think, Peter? You know what Whitney said, after I stopped that meeting cold? He said, 'Just don't take anything he tries to give you.' That's what Whitney said, to the word. Isn't it, Lucy?" Throughout this he mixed a Deep South accent and precise English dizzyingly. And he had smiled from the start until now. Now his face was again a blank, his eyes flat and hard once more.

Peter started to withdraw the folder, but Carl reached for it suddenly, and said softly, "Don't you know the difference between me and Whitney, Peter? The difference is that I'm the boss." He took the folder and opened it.

For a long time he studied the sketches Peter had made. He looked at the map with his lips pursed, then returned it to the folder along with the sketches. He turned and looked out the window of the bus. They jolted to a stop, the motor rumbled and coughed, and they jerked into motion again. People got on. People got off. A child cried softly, was taken away. The driver looked at them curiously in the rear-view mirror. A drunk mumbled, dozed, mumbled, and finally lurched to the exit and left. And still Carl was silent.

The bus seemed abysmally cold. Peter closed his eyes and hunched down low trying to conserve his body heat. He shivered. They thought he might be a plant; perhaps this was the information the government was waiting for them to possess in order to spring into action against them. Carl had no way of knowing if Peter, Grange, Senator Roos had arranged this meeting, if it was the entrapment that seemed so inevitable. This involved the AEC, and atomic energy secrets were still the most sacred of all the cows in Washington.

Carl thought suddenly of his father and his scores of books about upper-middle-class white men and women in their plush apartments, adulterous, larcenous, enviable white people who couldn't be trusted to carry out the garbage. The novels had made his father a rich man, an unknown, never seen, rich man. Who used a talent to produce trash. It seemed to him suddenly that he was involved in one of the strange, Never-Never-Land plots that had made his father's books automatic best-sellers, Hollywood material. He stared out the window and knew that no matter if this was a plot, he would have to use the

material, and even that seemed out of one of the books
that he always read, hating every word, every hypocritical
impulse that had created them.

Carl looked at Peter, who was sitting hunched down,
apparently chilled although the bus was rather too warm.
A sick boy, he thought. Where did he fit in? There was no
answer. It could be that Peter was cooperating with the
senator, Grange, all of them, out of revenge. As soon as
the thought formed, Carl denied it. But on another level
he knew that his denial didn't erase the fact that white men
did get revenge on black men who slept with white
women. Nothing political about it. Pure and simple
revenge. Where did Peter fit in? He drew his thoughts
back to the folder and knew that he had to come to some
kind of a decision, and he knew there was no way he could
decide without dragging in his personal reactions to
Peter, to Lucy. And finally what it came to was the
question: Did he have any reason to trust Peter? He
almost smiled, and looked at the window that showed his
reflection, an ugly black man, asking himself if he trusted
a pretty white boy. The smile twisted into a grimace.

Suddenly Peter sat upright, his shivering stopped, and
now he felt almost feverish. "Lucy, remember that last
time that we were at Grange's house? You, Wesselman,
Simon, Stein, me. That's what Grange is worried about,
Lucy. That's why he had to get rid of you, keep you from
remembering. That's why our whole damn class of
graduate students flunked out one way or another."

Lucy was staring at him in bewilderment. She shook
her head. "There wasn't anything."

Peter was perspiring and he knew he was talking too
fast, that it made no sense to either of the other two.
"There was a storm suddenly, and we rushed in from the
garden, in through the nearest doors. Wesselman took
Grange in through the front door. Grange was in a
wheelchair. Remember? He had wrenched his back and
he was in a cast or something. Don't you remember? The
wind blew his papers off the desk, scattered them to hell
and gone, and we picked them up. You and I behind the
desk, trying to straighten them when Grange came

wheeling in through the doorway and he started to scream and yell like a madman. Something on that desk that we saw, or might have seen. Something that had no meaning to us then, but now..."

Carl was looking at him fixedly. The flatness of his eyes was disturbing; there was no hostility, no friendliness, nothing coming from him. A blank wall. It was as if for his entire life he had lived among people that he had to shield himself against, to hide from. And he had learned to do it automatically now. He was so far back from his skin that even if he were flayed, Peter thought, the real Carl Davis would not be touched at all. He thought of the real Carl Davis as a many-faceted gem buried deep inside this man, untouchable for ever and ever. Carl said, "I should think, Brer Peter, that with the material you just gave me, you wouldn't need to go back to anything else in order to have Grange hot on your tail."

"But there's no way on earth for anyone to have that material. He knows that stuff is safe with him. He couldn't be worried about it. It's the other thing that made him let me be drafted, that made him try to frame Lucy on a bummer. Made Simon end up teaching high-school science. We all might have seen something on his desk that day. Something important for him." And that was why they wanted him put away now, he realized. Grange must have reasoned that Lucy hadn't seen anything, or had forgotten completely, but Peter, with his memory returning bit by bit, he was the unknown factor. Safer to put him away, pump him first, then simply keep him put away.

Lucy closed her eyes, frowning. "An article with footnotes. I seem to remember the footnotes, because they were always such a pain to space, you know."

"Not that," Peter said impatiently. "Something private. Correspondence, or notes, something like that. Dunnock," He said suddenly. "A letter to Dunnock."

Carl was looking out the window again, and abruptly he said, "Look, children, we are being followed, have been followed from the time we met. Peter, could you reproduce those sketches?" Peter nodded. "Because I'm afraid that I've been careless with matches again," Carl said softly. He crumbled the papers from the folder and let them fall to the side of his seat, screened from the driver by his body. Lucy moved slightly, farther from the window, closer to Peter. Carl lighted a cigarette and let the match fall to the papers. No one looked at it. After a moment Carl said softly, "Lucy, baby, why don't you scream, and you and Peter clog up the aisle a little bit while I wrestle with this conflagration that some careless idiot started?"

Lucy's hysteria was less than convincing to Peter, but they managed to keep the driver away from the rear of the bus long enough to allow Carl to dance around the fire a few minutes, and finally stamp the ashes into dust. They were all evicted right there, in the middle of a dark street. The driver watched them with disgust until they moved to the sidewalk, and then he drove off.

The cars that had been following the bus had vanished. Parked without lights, waiting to see what they would do next, Peter thought. Someone would get on the bus at the next stop, pry among the ashes, learn nothing. They started to walk.

"What will we do now?" Lucy asked.

"Walk to the nearest bar, or drugstore, or whatever and call a cab," Carl said lightly.

"You know I don't mean that."

Ahead of them, two car lengths away, a car door opened and a dark figure stepped out. "Hey, you people want a ride?" It was Norman Pryor.

"You see?" Carl said softly. "Providence always provides." He raised his voice slightly. "Mr. Pryor, what a pleasure to run into you. Thank you, we accept your kind offer."

In the back seat of Pryor's car, Peter shivered and felt feverish alternately. In his peripheral vision Lucy shimmered, flashed on and off in glowing lights.

Pryor drove slowly, without talking for a block or two, then he looked at Carl and said, "Just what the hell were you doing on that bus? It looked like a voodoo dance of some sort."

"A voodoo dance," Carl said.

They had turned onto a busier street and abruptly Pryor made a left turn, cutting across traffic. After another few seconds he said cheerfully, "You guys know that you've got an assortment of tails, don't you?" He chuckled. "Looks like a Goddamn circus parade." No one answered and he started to whistle softly. He was not trying to lose anyone following; he drove slowly and carefully now so that the followers would have no trouble in keeping up. After several more blocks, he said, "Any place in particular, or you just want to sightsee?"

"Home," Peter said.

"I don't think so, Peter, old buddy," Pryor said cheerfully. "Unless you want to be served with a summons or something. What do they call a certification procedure anyway? Never thought about the terminology."

"Certification!" Lucy whispered. "What do you mean?"

"They want to put your boy away, honey. They got the doctors, and the lawyer to make it legal, and the judge to give it his blessing. Everything in apple-pie order, just waiting for him to show."

"Mr. Pryor," Carl said, and his voice, while still low, was not gentle now, but hard and somehow flat, the way his eyes could become. "What's your interest in any of this?"

Peter was trying desperately to think of where he could go. Not S.A.F.E. headquarters. A hotel? Someplace where he could reproduce the sketches, rest, evade Raitt. At least long enough to find out if the map location meant anything.

Pryor drove another block before he answered Carl's question. "I wanted my man to have a talk with Peter," he said. "Word got out that S.A.F.E. is being put out of business, that you people are being charged with something, and I thought a senator's brother would be good story material. Imagine my surprise when I learned that my man walked into a mess of operators, all waiting for Peter to show up. I wanted to see for myself and got there in time to see Peter walk out with the young lady and a procession of others fall in line behind them. They didn't have the court order yet. They have it now. How interesting, I thought. So I got in line too." His voice was so light, so amused, and underlying it, so curious and hard. He continued, "Of course the young lady had her own follower. And you, Mr. Davis, when you drove up, had yours. As I said, quite a procession. Made me expect ticker tape, or a band, or some damn thing at any moment."

"I don't understand," Lucy said suddenly, her voice high and shaky. "Why do they want you back in the hospital so badly?"

Peter hesitated a moment, then said, "Raitt is a psychiatrist, specializes, I think in interrogation. They needed a shrink to certify me, Krump couldn't do it, or wouldn't."

Pryor nodded. "Right. Why, Peter? What do you have that makes them bring in a big boy like Raitt?"

Lucy's fingers dug into Peter's arm and he sighed.

"Nothing," Peter said. "I'm a mental case. It's for my own good."

Pryor whistled tunelessly and continued to drive slowly.

"Back to S.A.F.E. headquarters," Lucy said softly, her voice tight and desperate. Her fingers were still hard on Peter's arm. He shook his head. "We have to go somewhere, Peter. We won't let them in for you."

He shook his head again. "Take us home with you, Pryor," he said. "I think we can deal."

"No!" Lucy cried. "He doesn't have anything for us!"

"But, Peter," Pryor said amusedly, "what makes you think I want to tangle with Raitt and his boys?"

Peter shivered hard. "You'll get a story," he said.

Lucy pulled her hand away from Peter's arm and put both hands in her pockets. She looked straight ahead. "You'd sell us out?"

The cold increased. Carl said, "Leave him alone, Lucy. What's Raitt going to get from you, Peter?"

"I don't know," Peter said wearily. "A fishing expedition. The map, the sketches, for openers. When you fish and get a strike you keep on fishing in the same waters. They would want to know about your paper, sources, how it is financed, what else you support. Where you have spent your father's money." He could sense Pryor's attention, excitement now. "Pryor could help," he said slowly, his voice sounding distant even to him. "He has an inside man at AEC." Pryor swerved and cursed briefly. "Eberhardt," Peter said, drawing it from the darkness that was inhumanly cold. He shut his eyes.

Chapter 19

Pryor's apartment achieved a rich, and surprising, effect through contrasts: brilliant, fiery red drapes, white carpeting; a glass cabinet of first editions, and crystal in every conceivable shape, animals, fish, birds, free-form statues, an obelisk on a black pedestal; antique furniture side by side with chrome and plastic.

"Crystal is nice," Pryor said, as they entered, "because unlike most sculpture, it has not only surface, but depth as well. Your eye is drawn inward in spite of yourself, inward, through, stopped by a glare, only to search to find another entrance. Almost hypnotic."

The man who had admitted them looked like a weight lifter, or a boxer. He stood waiting. "No one's had dinner? Right?" Pryor asked. "Make up a platter of sandwiches, drinks, coffee," he told the man. He looked very much at home here, his hand trailed over the sensuous material lovingly, his eyes caressed his statuary, his rare books. All his art was tactile, Peter realized. No paintings at all, only things he could feel.

"Let me show you to the room you will use tonight," Pryor said. "You and your friends can have a conference." Lucy looked at him and he smiled and said, almost maliciously, "It's not bugged. I don't eavesdrop on my guests." He led them from the spacious room, through a hallway with half a dozen doors, to the end, where he opened the door and motioned them through. The bedroom was luxurious and impersonal. "I'll be in the living room," he said and left them.

Lucy closed the door and stood with her back to it. "What are you up to?" Carl moved past Peter and sat down on one of two chairs in the room.

Peter was very tired. His legs felt leaden, and the dull

headache was still there. He sat on the bed and leaned against the headboard. "I don't know," he said finally. "I'm not up to much, to tell the truth. Raitt tried to give me a lie detector test in the hospital, claimed it was routine. I walked out."

"You're protecting your brother!"

He shook his head. "No. He's in it, whatever it is. I couldn't protect him if I wanted to. I need time. I have to find out if the map is legitimate. If the site is actually where they are building the prototype city."

Lucy made a rude noise and turned her back to him very deliberately.

Peter closed his eyes. He said, "I went to see Grange. After our talk, in the hall outside his door, I overheard him on the telephone. He mentioned a site. Maybe I saw that map back four years ago in his office. Maybe somewhere else. I don't know. I don't know if it's true. I have great blanks in my memory still. Can't you trust me, Lucy?"

"Trust!" she said bitterly. "You overheard Grange! He just happened to be on the phone, saying just what you wanted to hear! And on the day we got a tip about you! And now you just happened to need a place to hide and Pryor just happened to come along! You're still trying to bail out your brother! You always thought he was ten feet tall! You got your head blown off so he wouldn't be embarrassed! And now you're selling us out to that Goddamn fairy!"

"It isn't our story, Lucy, baby," Carl said. "We wanted to give it to everybody, remember? If we're enjoined, then Pryor can do it for us, if he's interested. The important thing is to get it published. Right?"

"He already smells a Pulitzer," she said bitterly. "Your Pulitzer."

"If that's the carrot, so be it," Carl said. "Let's go eat the man's sandwiches, and drink his booze and coffee and talk. Then I'll go home and see if the law is there. Okay?"

She nodded, her expression still resentful. Then quickly she said, "I'm coming with you. I don't want to stay here tonight."

Carl glanced at Peter, "Whatever you say, Lucy."

The sandwiches were ready, and a bar had been set up. Pryor was on the white couch with a sandwich. "Just help yourselves, sit where you want, drink what you want." He was drinking black coffee.

Lucy didn't look at the table. She sat in a straight chair near the window, as far from the couch as the room permitted. For the next hour Peter and Carl filled in the details of the underground city project, answered questions, and Peter pinpointed the site he had visualized on a state map. Pryor made no notes. From time to time he looked at Peter curiously, but he didn't ask for his sources of information.

"I called a couple of guys who work for me," he said finally. "If you'll excuse me, I'll just go talk to them. I'll have someone at the site by daylight," he said.

Lucy stood up. "We'll be going. You ready, Carl?"

He stood up too, but paused to look at Peter. "Are you all right?"

Peter said he was all right. Carl seemed to know he was lying, and for the first time the blank wall didn't seem so solid, the flat eyes seemed to deepen. Carl hesitated a moment longer, then he nodded. "See you in the morning," he said. He turned to Pryor. "You mind?"

Pryor shook his head. "Nope. Thought you might like to be on hand for the follow-up. See you." He left and they were shown out by the ex-fighter, or weight lifter.

Peter drank coffee and read and looked out the window until it seemed impolite to remain in the living room longer, then he went to his room. He was aware of the houseman all the time, not in sight, but nearby. Keeping an eye on him? He didn't know, didn't care. For hours there was activity in the large apartment. People came, left. The phone rang, muted by distance and doors.

Peter imagined Lucy, sitting crosslegged on a bed, talking earnestly to Carl, listening to him with trust. And he thought of Ed, lying sleepless, hands under his head, beside a wife whose life was a waste and who refused to see the wreckage about her.

Ed, so often betrayed by the earth he yearned for. First

the mine that burned for twenty-five years, that still burned and smoldered, and poisoned the air above it. That had been Ed's and his father's and uncle's mine, Peter knew. No one had ever told him, but he knew. Twenty-six men dead, a township destroyed. And years later the bomb shelter. Ed, so certain that the crisis was at hand, certain enough to seek safety for himself and his family, again in the earth, deep under the old barn. Moldering cans of peaches and tuna, that was the end of that chapter. And now, once more, seeking refuge in the earth, seeing ruin this time for himself and everyone else. Looking for a shelter all his life, finding ruins.

At seven Peter returned to the living room to find Pryor there with coffee and a doughnut. "Morning. Breakfast?" Pryor asked. He waved the doughnut. "I know they're bad for me. Poisonous things, do nothing but add cholesterol and calories, but I can't resist. Every morning for forty-three years. My only vice."

Peter had coffee. He couldn't tell if Pryor had slept or not. He looked exactly the same—soft, languorous, effeminate, ineffectual. Until you looked at his eyes, Peter thought, and they were the eyes of a snake, veiled, secret, wise.

At nine-thirty Pryor's man from upper New York State called and confirmed that major construction was taking place. He and three others were going in for a closer look, and they would report. Pryor was satisfied. They had given him the name of the construction firms on the job. One man would be arrested, one would be chased, and one would get through, he said to Peter. And the one that got through? Peter asked. Pryor gave him a quizzical look. He'd get a job there, of course.

The day was slow. Pryor was in and out of the living room, to his office, to his study, back to the living room. For several hours a typewriter clacked professionally. A secretary, Peter thought, listening to it. Pryor had introduced him to no one, no one had come into the living room. He doesn't know you, Pryor had said about his houseman. No one's introduced you to him. He doesn't know your name. He can honestly say you're not here. Of course, if anyone describes you and asks for you that way, we'll discover how very poor his eyesight is too.

Raitt called. Pryor said the men were still downstairs, confined to the lobby, but that there was talk about a search warrant. He looked at Peter curiously. "You stepped right on that hornet's nest, didn't you?"

Late in the afternoon Lucy and Carl returned. Lucy's eyes were dark-circled, and she was pale and nervous. Everyone at S.A.F.E. had been arrested, there had been a preliminary hearing already and they were out on bail. The paper was closed down.

"There's construction," Pryor told Carl. "Much too much for an electrical power plant. And it seems that they have run into major difficulties with it. We're not sure what kind of trouble yet."

"Do you have a geologist?" Carl asked. Pryor shook his head. "I have a friend over at M.I.T.," Carl said. "He'd be our boy."

Lucy stood up. "Peter can I talk to you?" She didn't wait for an answer, but walked toward the door, toward his room where he had not slept the night before. Inside, she turned to look at him, and again she seemed remote, strange, under tight control. "How did you find out about Carl's father?"

"I don't know."

"You know. Tell me, Peter. It's important. No one knew about him, about the money. If they have checked that thoroughly we should know about it."

"Nothing's hidden that well," Peter said impatiently. "If it's on record anywhere, it's available. If he has anything that can jump out of the past, they'll use it eventually to discredit him. He knows that."

"You said you knew about the money, other money. What did you mean?"

"Ask Carl."

"I'm asking you."

"No, Lucy."

She wheeled about and went to the window, moving jerkily. When she looked at him again, she was very pale, her voice was faint. "Carl thinks you got that out of his mind, that no one told you anything. That AEC name you pulled out. His past. Dunnock. That map." She looked cold.

Peter sat down and didn't say anything. She could use him, he thought, and wished she would say it. They could use him. He would be invaluable to them. If he could do it. And if he could do it, she was terrified of him. Monstrous. Intolerable.

"I don't know where I got any of that stuff," he said. "I don't know how much of what I know is real knowledge, how much is revived memory, how much is fantasy. There are no edges any longer. Can you understand what I'm saying?"

She shook her head, afraid, watching him with her very large eyes that seemed blind, wide open, aimed, seeing nothing.

"Lucy..."

"Don't look at me," she whispered. "Just don't look at me!"

He turned away and after a moment he heard her take a deep breath. Then another. He wondered if she had been faint, if she was fighting hysteria. He didn't look at her.

"We have to get you out of here," she said. "Away from Raitt, your brother, Pryor. We can hide you away from them all."

"Is this what Carl wants?"

"I don't know what he wants. He says you need an operation. But they won't operate, will they? They'll use you, make you tell them everything you know, and then make you learn more and tell them that."

Away in a cabin somewhere, he thought. By the sea? In the mountains. He remembered the mountains, the tall trees that seemed to touch the sky, wandering hand in hand with Lucy, in the deep shade, breathing in the indefinable fragrance of the tall trees. Silence that was eerie. They had been frivolous earlier, gaily talking about the wood spirits that had been forced to retreat more and more until now they existed in these small enclaves. And walking, not talking, hand in hand, something had happened to them. Simultaneously they had stopped, frightened, awed, moved? He couldn't then explain what had happened, he couldn't now. I felt it, Lucy had whispered moments later, pale and frightened, very, very high. And he, as high, exalted as he could ever hope to be again, he had felt it too. They had made love under the trees, feeling the blessing of the spirit on them, and afterwards they had been subdued and even reverent.

"We'll find a way to smuggle you out past Raitt's men," she said.

"Lucy, will you go away with me? Just the two of us?"

"I can't."

"They have everything they need. It's up to Pryor now, and Carl and the people he knows. Back to the mountains, Lucy, to rest, think..."

"No!" she cried. And she put her hands over her face and shook. "Don't look at me!"

He went to her and took her in his arms. She was trembling, distant. He was holding a stranger. Silently he released her and went to the door. "Anything else?"

She shook her head and he left her alone.

Pryor's look was searching when Peter returned. "Raitt is here," he said. "I parked him in another room. We can't stall them any longer, Peter. He has a search warrant. Do you want to talk to him?"

"Why not?"

Raitt looked as much at home in the sophisticated apartment as Pryor did, Peter thought. Raitt would blend in anywhere. He shook Peter's hand briefly. "Can we talk?"

"Sure." Peter sat down on the long white couch and waited.

"I mean in private."

"No more secrets, Dr. Raitt. There's no need for secrecy. Mr. Pryor tells me you have a search warrant."

Raitt looked at him with a helpless smile and shrugged his thin, sloping shoulders. "It's out of my hands, Peter. Once it's in the legal department, there's little anyone can do about it."

"Why?" Lucy demanded from the doorway. Her eyes

were red-rimmed now. "Why do you want him back so Goddamned much?"

Raitt stood up and looked from her to Peter. He introduced them. Raitt said, "Peter, with an injury like yours, there is a definite danger that a psychosis could develop with another attack. You simply must be under observation until we can determine the proper course of treatment."

"Let him go to a private doctor!" Lucy demanded.

"It's too late for that now, I'm afraid," Raitt said smoothly. "You see, the court order has already been signed. As I said, once it gets in the legal department, there's really very little anyone can do about it."

"Why are you here?" Carl said softly. "You have the machinery to go ahead and do it, it seems."

"I don't want a public fuss," Raitt said, still smiling his helpless-little-boy grin. "Mr. Pryor's retaliatory powers are well known to us, so we decided a commonsense, practical course of frankness would be our best approach."

Peter looked at Lucy and she jerked away from his glance. Don't look at me! Don't see me! Don't know me! You can touch me and I won't even know you're there! Every mean, vicious, vile thought, and I'll never know you're there! Don't look at me!

The apartment was cold and the contrast of the red and white in the room was making his eyes hurt, and the vision at both edges was so bright it was as if spotlights were turned on in the wings, highlighting the stage, making the side entrances and exits dance in shimmering colors. For a moment Peter's gaze caught Carl's, and the look they exchanged was thoughtful, and, Peter realized, filled with pity from Carl, pity, compassion, understanding when understanding was impossible, and even the beginnings of affection. Carl's eyes really had changed, he thought with surprise, they were no longer flat, cold, impenetrable disks. And his expression was open, responsive. Raitt said something and Carl turned to look at him. Raitt spoke again, and Peter knew he was being spoken to. He seemed very far from it all, cold and alone and far away.

"Are you all right?" Raitt asked again.

"Sure. I'm tired, and achy, and edgy, and I want nothing on this earth more than just to be left alone. I won't go with you, Raitt. Not willingly. If you try any coercion, you'll precipitate an attack. You know that. I know it."

For a moment Raitt hesitated, then he said, "Another attack will more than likely kill you, Peter. I know Krump would kill you in surgery. That's an inoperable area. You know that, too. I might save your life. That's the choice."

Lucy looked desperately afraid now; she was so rigid that every muscle must have become tensed. She would be sore and never know why.

Peter closed his eyes. The dancing, glowing lights were too hard to take. Somewhere it seemed a door opened, and the surge of frigid air made him shiver. He was swamped by hatred, malice, fear, contempt. Peter couldn't tell whose emotions they were, but they were all there. It seemed that they were all talking at him, thinking at him together and he couldn't separate out the voices, the thoughts, couldn't make them stop. He tried to reach Lucy, and she eluded him, emitting waves of fear that were hurtful, damaging. He felt that he was slipping away from the man on the couch, Peter, slipping away from him, unable to feel his hands and feet, aware that the numbness was creeping up the legs of that distant man. *Move!* He was being driven out of that man by the others, he thought with dispassionate interest. They were too many, too charged to resist, and he was being driven farther and farther out where it was very cold and black. *Move!* They were killing him, he thought and felt amazement at the helplessness of the man on the couch. His lover, his protector, his friend, his doctor, they were killing him. *Move!* He visualized a door and tried to hold steady an image of himself standing at the door, reaching for it. The image shivered before him and faded. The noise inside his skull increased and he thought, noise brought on the headache. He formed the image again and lost it. Drifting so far away now that it seemed impossible to return to the couch, to the man slowly going numb, ebbing away. Again, the man, Peter, stood at the door, reaching for the knob, grasping it finally. The image shook and divided into segments. He held it and forced the pieces together and he hung on from millions of miles away, a place where it was quiet and there were no noises, no thoughts. He clung to the doorknob and didn't know why he was doing it now. He turned it and the door opened, and he swung it shut hard, feeling its bang like an explosion in his head.

Lucy was talking about calling in a private doctor, holding off the process servers for another hour. Raitt didn't look at her. He was watching Peter closely. "I don't think we should waste any more time," he said, and now his tone was authoritative. He stood up.

Pryor's houseman appeared in the doorway. "Telephone for Mr. Roos," he said. "Senator Roos is calling."

"Put it through in Mr. Roos' bedroom," Pryor said. The man nodded and vanished.

Peter followed him through the doorway into the wide hall, and then he paused. The man had vanished, the others were talking again, heatedly, all together.

Suddenly he knew he was not going to talk to Ed. He was not going to return to the clamorous room he had just left. He picked up a coat in the hallway and opened a door and went outside the apartment to a wide corridor. An elevator was standing open, he entered and pushed number 2. It seemed to be an interminable ride. At the second floor he left the elevator and walked the length of the corridor to an exit sign and went down the stairs the rest of the way, emerging from the building through a side entrance. His luck seemed extraordinary, a cab was discharging a passenger at the curb. He hailed it and sat down inside all in an instant. And then he didn't know where he could go. The driver turned to look at him inquiringly, and Peter finally told him the name of the street that Senator Thomas Knute lived on. He couldn't remember the number. He closed his eyes wearily. If Tom wasn't home, so much the better, he would wait for him and rest and think.

Chapter 20

Tom was home. He was surprised and happy to see Peter. "I just brought Janice home," Tom said, "How did you know I'd be here?"

"I didn't. I needed somewhere to go and this came to mind. How is Janice?"

"I don't know," Tom said after a brief hesitation. "Deep depression. She's afraid the baby was hurt, I think. She won't say. Or can't. They thought it might help to have her here where she can see the children, reassure her that everything is going to be normal again. But she wants them to stay with their grandparents. I just don't know."

He looked very tired. He sat down in a worn leather chair and studied Peter openly.

"Whatever it is, you can tell me," he said after a moment. "You know that. And I would appreciate it. I'm going out of my skull worrying about Janice, trying to hide it from her. It's like hiding a boil on your nose from your mother, you realize."

Peter grinned and sat down. And he started. An hour later he finished, and Tom sat motionless, staring at nothing in particular, no expression on his face.

"You mind if I call Ed, ask him over?" Tom asked after a minute or two. Peter shook his head.

"He knows there are city plans," Peter said. "He saw them once. And he knows there is a partnership involving General Ford, Senator Dukes, Marko, Grange." He shook his head again. "I don't think he appreciates how far it's gone." He stared at the floor, then added, "I don't care if he comes over or not. He'll deny it, of course, and warn you that I'm crazy."

Tom nodded. "He might." He dialed, holding his hand

over the phone, he said, "He's been an awfully good friend to me, Peter."

"He's my brother," Peter said.

Tom was connected to Ed's office, and spoke briefly with a secretary. Ed was out. He returned the call almost immediately. "I have to see you as soon as possible," Tom said. Ed must have protested; his voice grew harder, and he said distinctly, "It's of vital interest to you personally, Ed. And it's urgent. I'm home."

"Two hours," he said to Peter, gently cradling the phone again. "I'll go see if Janice would like a visitor, okay? It might cheer her up."

"You trust me to cheer her up?" Peter asked incredulously.

"Don't be an ass," Tom said. "Be right back."

Moments later Tom led Peter to an upstairs room and tapped lightly on a door. He pushed it open without waiting for an answer. Janice was in bed. There was a cast on one arm, up to her shoulder. She looked very ill, her face white and pinched, deep circles under her eyes, her eyelids red and swollen. Peter went to the side of her bed and sat down awkwardly on a straight chair.

"How lovely to see you," Janice said, and her voice was what he remembered, low, husky. Somehow the sound of her voice brought back the other Janice and he smiled at her and found himself reaching for her hand.

Janice's hand was cold and trembled slightly. She took it back hastily. But her gaze stayed on Peter's face and suddenly she said, still looking at Peter, "Tom, would you mind leaving us a minute or two? Would you mind?"

Tom kissed her forehead and left them without a word.

"Peter, I'm going to ask a favor of you. It's very important to me. He mustn't know. Please, Peter. Please!"

She was near hysteria, he thought, and he nodded. "Anything at all."

She swallowed hard and said, "In a desk downstairs, a room off the kitchen, my study, office, I don't know what it is, but it's my room, my desk. The bottom left-hand drawer. There is a box with letters in it. Please bring them up here, and burn them for me. I have to know they're destroyed, that he won't find them."

Peter stood up. "No one will try to stop me, or anything like that?"

"Say I sent you for them. I don't think anyone will interfere." She was watching him intently, and when he nodded, she took a deep breath and closed her eyes.

He hurried downstairs to find the room and the box of letters. He tried not to think what must be in the letters.

"Read one," she demanded when he returned with the box.

He picked one off the top and opened it. It was typewritten, well done, neat, grammatical. And it dripped hate and poison. He glanced at her and picked up a second one. The same. Bitch. Sow. Kid factory. Worse. "Are they all like that?" he asked.

She nodded. "I've been getting them for months. I kept telling myself that the writers are sick, that they're the real fanatics, that they don't represent any real opinion, but they kept coming. So full of hate." Her face twisted and she turned her head on the pillow. "Burn them. Please, Peter, burn them up."

"You should show them to Tom," he said hesitantly.

"No!" She could hardly move, but she attempted to sit up and he hurried to the bed and gently took her free hand.

"I promised," he said. "I'll do what I promised."

She relaxed. "You don't understand," she said. "Just get rid of them. I was so afraid he might find them. Or one of the children."

"Janice, you don't have to feel guilt over them," he said, his back to her, watching the first one curl up and blacken in the fireplace.

"But I do have to. I don't have the right to bring any more children into the world. My child will consume enough to keep forty, fifty Indians alive. All that is true. I don't have the right."

"And if your child, because of you and Tom and what you can give him, turns out to be an artist, or an inventor, or a surgeon who saves lives routinely? Doesn't that count?"

"You don't understand," she repeated. "They hate me. Those boys who knocked me down and took my purse, they hated me. One of them kicked me in the stomach. All over the world there are people who hate us like that. In this country. I thought I would ask Marie, my maid, to get the box, and I looked at her and wondered if she hated me. If she might not have written one of those letters. I couldn't ask her to do anything for me."

Peter threw the last three letters into the fire and stood up with the box in his hands. With a feeling of disgust for it and its lingering taint, he tossed it in, too. He went back to the bedside and stood looking at Janice helplessly. She was weeping softly.

"All our lives," she said in a thick, choking voice, "we kept saying we wanted our children to have it better than we had it. You know. Better everything. And now, God, how I pray they'll have it as good as we did. Just not too much worse."

He held her cold hand and there was nothing he could say.

She would bear the child, he thought, alive or dead, and she would go into analysis and a doctor, or a series of doctors, would try to get her to accept hatred as one of the human emotions, to accept that she would have to be the target of such hatred from time to time. And maybe they would dismiss her, "cure" her, but they would never, never bring to life that something that had been murdered within her. She looked at him, her eyes filled with tears, and he leaned over and kissed her on the forehead, as Tom had done.

"Peter, thank you. Perhaps I can sleep now. I couldn't knowing those vile things were in the house. And the doctor is afraid of pills this late in pregnancy. Thank you, Peter."

He nodded and left quietly.

"I just can't believe it," Tom said, pacing, looking at his watch. The two hours Ed had allowed himself were up, and in the past ten minutes Tom had looked at the watch half a dozen times. Janice was napping.

"But if it all does check out?" Peter asked. "Then what?"

Tom sat down once more and stared moodily at Peter. "Then I join in the destruction of my best friend. I make a big stink and start investigations of the site you located for your friend Davis. I start poking into the AEC, with all the reverberations that will cause. I'll find out who's been paying the bills. Push to cut off funds. Check Ford's connection with it. There will be a full-scale Senate investigation, hearings, subpoena powers. Grand jury proceedings. The works." He rubbed his eyes hard. "The AEC! Christ!"

"How much proof will you need?"

"I don't know. First I want to talk to Ed. Then I'll know." He stared at Peter for a long time. "Janice says you are all right," he said finally. "Not crazy, on the level. She says you're awfully unwell, too. Are you?"

"Yes."

"She knows these things," Tom said. "I've always trusted her without question, and she's always been right. She wanted you to get rid of the letters, didn't she?"

Peter nodded, not surprised that Tom had known about them.

"I couldn't tell her I knew," Tom said, "because she was working so desperately hard to keep it a secret. Thanks," he added. Peter nodded and they sat quietly for several minutes. Then Tom said, his voice vehement, "She's lost something, and I have too. We won't get it back. And I keep thinking there's got to be something we can do. I don't know what yet, but I swear to God, I'm going to try my damnedest to find out. Not more laws. We have enough. What?"

Peter waited. Tom was thinking out loud, he knew, he didn't want any answers, comments.

"I'm going to fight this DEDF thing as hard as I can," Tom said after a moment. "Good men will be hurt, some of them destroyed, some institutions might crumble. That's the starting place. Clean up our own street and then start on the neighborhood, one block at a time. But first our own house." He drank his bourbon and water and scowled at the glass. "He should be here."

When Ed arrived Tom and Peter were shaken at his appearance; he was gray-faced and ill looking. He paled even more when he saw Peter.

"For God's sake!" he cried, "everyone in the city is looking for you! Raitt thought you had had another attack, that you might be on the street somewhere unconscious or dead."

"He's been here for hours," Tom said quietly. "We've been talking about Grange and his project. Sit down, Ed. Drink?"

Ed nodded and when Tom put the drink in his hand he gulped it. "Peter, they're looking for you as a dangerous psychotic! A psychotic! The police are looking for you!" A new thought struck him and he put his glass down shakily. "Oh, my God!" he muttered. "They'll think we arranged to meet here."

Tom looked sick. He stared at a point over Ed's shoulder without speaking for several seconds and then said quietly, "How deeply into it are you, Ed?"

Ed shrugged. "Enough. I didn't start out knowing how far it would go. They needed someone on the Atomic Energy Committee to push through the appropriations for exploratory field work in the Eric area. So help me God, that's what I thought. There've been cost overruns, but there have been on all the power plant projects. Last year I began to realize how much further they meant to go before it came into the open. There wasn't anything I could do by then." He spoke harshly without looking at Peter. "Grange talked to me. He took me in completely. The Rockies are honeycombed, there was no danger. A simple construction job, and the power plant was already on the books. And if the crisis did come, we would be able to save something. The government anyway, our military capacity to strike back, enough technology to start again—if it got that bad. He was plausible then."

"Plausible enough to make you agree to risk criminal action if this came to light?" Peter asked.

"It won't come to light," Ed said. "There isn't anything to come to light. There is an atomic plant being built. Period. Some people are pushing for a study of underground facilities for defense purposes. Period. That's all that can come to light."

Peter shook his head. "I know about the city, Ed. And the location of the site. There will be correspondence. People always keep it to protect themselves if for no other reason. And people will fall all over themselves to talk once it hits the fan. They always do. Pryor's got it, too, Ed. And he won't let go. You know that."

Ed stared at him. "You've been spying for them! Ford said you were a spy!"

"Ed, just quietly, here with no one who's going to repeat it in court, nothing at all like that, please tell me why?"

For a moment Ed stiffened, then he sagged again and his voice was muffled when he spoke. "I don't know. My God, I just don't know. I believed Grange. I do believe we're heading for a crisis, a confrontation that will destroy the world civilization. It's true, there's no way to avoid it. It's there before us, as inevitable as old age. You can't convince people of this. They think you're neurotic, paranoid. But it's true! And we're helpless to do anything to avert it. The only thing we can do is try to save something." As he spoke his voice gained in volume, as if he were selling himself all over again. Now he looked at Peter almost defiantly. "And yes, by God, I was ready to go to jail for what I was doing, if it came to that! I believed in what I was doing! I believed it would be a good thing for this country, if we could save just part of it if a real emergency came. And it's coming."

Peter nodded. Grange could make you believe it snowed in hell every Thursday. "And the crisis? A military showdown? A mistaken attack?" He stopped, chilled, and said slowly. "They will engineer the crisis, won't they? The Cuban crisis all over again, this time with no pull-out at the last minute?"

Tom stood up abruptly and looked at Ed in disbelief. "That's the missing piece," he said slowly. "If there's a crisis of that magnitude who's going to ask any questions? They'll be too busy pinning on medals, won't they?"

Ed buried his face in his hands. "I don't know," he said thickly. "And there's no need. If they'll just wait, they won't have to manufacture anything at all."

Tom was pacing, muttering softly. "A crisis that lasts ten years? Time enough to go ahead with half a dozen more underground complexes? Something like that surely. Not a sudden blowup. Heat it all up again and keep it boiling, push through emergency powers. And by then we're committed to it. That must be it. Ford! That tin-plated bastard! That's his contribution, isn't it?"

"It's Grange's baby," Peter said tiredly. "He had the idea five years ago, or even longer. He's the one who masterminded it from the start."

"There's not a shred of anything to link him," Ed said dully. "He made that clear to us this morning. With you out of it, Peter, and your flow of information from D. C., there is nothing to prove. I fired her. I'm to go away for a rest. Nervous exhaustion. They're getting rid of the excess baggage now. You. Me. There's nothing to prove. That hole in the ground can be explained. An atomic energy power plant. Sloppy work, but they ran into trouble. There's nothing."

Tom looked at Peter questioningly. Peter thought again of the letter that had been on Grange's desk a lifetime ago, the letter that he had seen, that Lucy had seen, even if she no longer remembered it. He hoped to God that Eberhardt was on Dunnock's tail. He shook his head at Tom. There was more. Ed wouldn't look at him. He said gently, "You know D. C. is loyal to you. She gave me nothing. You had a meeting. Was Raitt there?"

Ed nodded. His voice was low and dead when he spoke, "He told us you don't have a chance, Peter. It's killing you. That tumor, or whatever it is. And before you die, you'll probably go mad." A tremor passed through him, but still he didn't look up.

"Does that give them the authority to shoot me on sight, Ed?" Peter asked, still gently. "You can pull out, Ed. Now. Before it goes any further. Meetings, people, dates.

Notes on the meetings. You were duped, taken in by Grange."

Ed looked at him as if at a stranger. He shook his head. "Political suicide," he said thickly. "I might as well cut my own throat."

Peter reached out and put his hand on Ed's shoulder. Ed jerked away violently.

Peter stared at him a moment, then started toward the door. "Thank you, Tom," he said.

"Don't leave," Tom said quickly, coming to him.

Peter thought of Janice upstairs, asleep now. "I'll stay in touch," he said. He went out to the hall where he had tossed his coat down, and he looked at the coat in puzzlement. It wasn't his. He hadn't noticed before. It was tan, a very good coat, he thought putting it on again. It was a fair fit. Tom followed him to the door, worried.

"Take my car," he said.

Peter shook his head. "Thanks." He kept thinking about the coat, how warm it was. Outside he paused and wondered how it had got so late. It was dusk, not very cold, calm. The coat felt good on his back. Lightweight. The houses on this street were very handsome, very expensive, he thought walking. Not much of them showed, only the high parts that were above the trees. There were many trees. Very old trees. The street was broad, with a curve that was gradual and attractive. The street lights were coming on, pale blue green, some of them peach-colored, but so faintly colored that it could have been his imagination. There were not many cars on the broad curved street. No children. All very quiet and dignified. The air was colder than he had thought at first; he put his hands in the coat's pockets, deep pile-lined pockets. A coat meant to be worn in the coldest of climates. His fingers closed over a metal object and he took it from the pocket and looked at it under one of the peach-colored lights. This close, the light didn't seem to have any color at all. The object was Lucy's identification bracelet that she never had liked, too heavy on her wrist. It had been worn smooth, he thought, and fingered it over and over. He put it back in the pocket and walked.

He walked another block or two, then turned to his right, toward a busier highway where there were lights from filling stations, shops. At the first station that had a pay phone he turned in and had to ask the attendant for change. The attendant was young, a smooth-faced boy with hair to his shoulders. Peter closed his eyes against the glare of the brightly lighted station. When he entered the phone booth, he was aware that the boy had come after him, that he was making work nearby. He must look pretty bad, Peter thought. He called Dr. Krump and while he waited for him to be located in the hospital, he leaned his head against the glass of the booth, no longer paying any attention if the boy was near or not. There was a throbbing in his temples, and a tightness about his head that regularly expanded and constricted. He had seen a taxi stand across the street. He would get a taxi and go to the nearest movie and stay for an hour and a half, and then he would go to the hospital.

"Dr. Krump? Yes, it's Peter. I'm starting another headache, and within three hours it will be critical, I suppose. If I am brought to you then, will you be allowed to treat me on an emergency basis?" The doctor asked questions and he answered very carefully, thinking again how warm Carl Davis's overcoat was, how smoothly the bracelet had been worn down. Finally he hung up and started to cross the street to the taxi stand. And he never even saw the car that appeared out of the twilight and sped toward him.

He lay with his head on the cold concrete, and above him there were voices, a siren, a gruff voice asking questions. Wearily Peter tried not to hear them, to return to sleep, but his mind refused to cooperate and he heard.

"Yeah, on his way to Walter Reed. I heard him on the phone, talking to his doctor. Jesus, I don't know the doctor's name."

"Thanks," Peter said to the boy. His words were smothered in the concrete that smelled of oil and dirt. "Thanks," he whispered again, and then he was being lifted, and something happened in his right shoulder, something seemed to snap with a fiery pain, and he lost consciousness again.

"Yeah, I'm telling you," the boy said, as they put Peter inside the ambulance. "The car was parked over there and it came barreling down like a bat, straight at him. I got the license number.

Chapter 21

Lights blinked off and on against Peter's closed lids, and irritably he wished they wouldn't do that. He looked up to tell them and he saw that the lights were ceiling lights that seemed to be moving past him. Gradually the movement became his, and he felt the table under him now, and to one side a dark hand holding an i.v. bottle. Ah, he thought, it wasn't on purpose, then, and he closed his eyes again. The table went over a bump, and he wanted to protest, but it was too much effort. An elevator. He felt that he had been in the hospital for an awfully long time. There were snatches of remembered procedures, but it was very confused; he couldn't tell if he was remembering from this time, or from the past.

He wished they had covered him with a blanket before wheeling him about the drafty halls. He wondered if they had looked at the overcoat, wondered if they had found lice on his body when they undressed him.

His mother had warned him, "They all have lice, you know." An image of Carl and Lucy flashed before his eyes and stayed there, and he couldn't get rid of it. His black hands on her smooth white belly, on her rounded breasts, the birthmark. Her legs opening for him. She trusted the son of a bitch, Peter knew, trusted him in a way that she never had trusted Peter. He couldn't imagine their fighting the way she had fought with him. She would never fear Carl the way she had come to fear Peter. Why? He wanted to ask her, and knew he never would. Why had she become afraid of him? Without asking her, he would never know. Something about him had frightened her finally. Something. He couldn't remember what it had been. He tried to find the bracelet, but his hands were not attached to him somehow.

The nurse finished shaving his head and a technician attached the electrodes and turned on the EEG. He was asking Peter questions, but Peter didn't want to talk now. He mumbled in answer, and knew that his mumbles were misleading—probably they thought he couldn't talk. He didn't care. Someone pressed him too hard on the right shoulder and he made a noise. He could have told the son of a bitch to lay off, he thought, but it seemed pointless. They were moving him again.

In the upper left corner of his room there was a right triangular patch perhaps three inches on its base, about four inches high, that was several shades darker than the walls. The walls were buff-colored from the floor to a molding; from there they were cream-colored to the ceiling. The ceiling was white. The triangular patch was noticeably darker than the pale walls. A too-full brush? A bowlegged Japanese painter slapping it on?

"Peter, dear, it's your mother and father."

"For God's sake, don't shake him!"

"I didn't. I just wanted to touch him. He's so pale. Peter! We didn't put him here, did we? It isn't our fault. I didn't want him to go into the army. You know I didn't. I don't like war any more than any mother does. I didn't want him in it. Will he think it's our fault?"

"For God's sake, just shut up, will you! Shut up! Being here is crazy. What damn good will it do him to cool our asses in this Goddamn waiting room? In a day or two they're going to put him in the ward. If we could do him any good..."

"Don't you let them do that. They're all colored in the ward."

"It won't make any difference to him. Can't you understand what I'm trying to tell you? He doesn't know anything."

There was something different about the operating room. Peter opened his eyes and saw two immense lights above him, big enough to swallow him. He shut his eyes hard. There was a feeling of purpose about the nurses and interns in the room that hadn't been present in the ones on duty in the emergency admitting office, or in the halls, or

the place where they had cleaned him and shaved him.
These people, he thought clearly, are not human.

Someone was doing something to his leg now, and
again he wanted to protest, but stubbornly clamped his
lips together. An inflatable splint, he thought, pumping
him up from the toes up, keeping him in place. His other
leg was being wrapped too, though, and he gave up trying
to puzzle out what they thought they were doing. There
were too many of them, each intent on an activity that
seemed incomprehensible to him. He heard his name and
opened his eyes reluctantly. Krump was there in a
rumpled soft green gown, his mask not on yet.

"I'm going to fix you, Peter," he said softly. And Peter
believed him. Dr. Krump nodded to a sexless green-
gowned doctor, or nurse, and Peter felt a needle in his
arm, and another voice saying, "Just breathe naturally,
Peter. We're giving you oxygen now." He saw the black
mask descending, and before it touched he closed his eyes
again. They didn't talk. There was no need. There was this
one animal, with dozens of pseudopods, each equipped to
do a special task. The guiding mind knew what each was
doing. Does one hand explain to the other its function?
These were Krump's hands, doing his will without
question. They were putting different sheets under him.
He was feverish. The sheets were very cold.

"Grange, are you there?" Peter knew he was. He
looked up and down the gray canyons, all empty. But he
was there. It was very cold; when the Ergs weren't needed,
they were deactivated, stored a few degrees above freezing
temperature. He could sense them, inert, thoughtless,
dreamless behind the gray walls. They weren't sending
any vibrations, nothing to interfere at all; he could home
in on Grange unimpeded by anything else.

He skimmed along the passageway, still following
something so elusive that he couldn't even tell which sense
to credit it to. This level was as functional and unadorned
as the interior of a freezer locker. He was going faster,
tilted forward, his feet above the gray surface of the
passage. Eight abreast could walk here. The light was

uniformly dim, but it didn't matter. There was nothing to
see. An intersection. Now he could look in four
directions, all exactly the same, corridors among the gray
shelves that they perhaps called apartments, storage space
for the Ergs. He hesitated a moment, then turned left. No
tangible reason for choosing this way. Only after he had
turned and gone a third of the way to the next intersection
did he see something different. The canyon walls rose
overhead, fifty stories high, higher maybe, unbroken by
windows or ornamentation. Not even marble, but a
gneiss, or granite smoothly cut, not finished more than
that. This was the industrial section where they manufac-
tured everything the city needed. Then a change.

Krump and his resident assistant studied the X rays
again, and looked at the electroencephalographs. "Those
damn spikes," Krump muttered and turned to scrub. He
was thinking of how it would have been if Peter had been
taken to a private hospital. They would have treated him
for shock, they would have set his leg, fixed his shoulder,
and when he died, they would have ascribed death to
shock. Or some resident idiot would have noticed the
plate in his head and would have gone in and killed him
outright. Without his X rays, without the recent tests, the
history, there would have been no chance of saving him.
Convulsion, paralysis, they would have gone into the
head. And that head was his, he thought vehemently.
There came a time, he thought, even more vehemently, to
say fuck the orders and go ahead and do the job that
needed doing. "Fuck the orders!" he said aloud, turning
to a nurse, who refused to be startled by anything he
might say.

There was a table in what appeared to be sunshine.
They all knew it wasn't really, but they pretended to be
fooled. D. C. wore very large, dark blue glasses, and Ed
squinted and perspired. The place was very busy. It was a
hybrid coffeehouse, restaurant, nightclub.

"Peter! An Irish coffee?"

"No thanks. Ed, I have to talk to you."

"Not now," D. C. said. "Leave him alone for a while.

Can't you? Look at him. He's looking five years younger, just relaxing, feeling happy." D. C. took off the dark glasses and glared at Peter. "For heaven's sake, Peter. There is no such thing as guiltlessness, innocence," she said. "You forfeit it when you grow up." The light faded.

Peter was turned face down and the anesthesiologist made an adjustment in her equipment. Krump glanced at her and she nodded. Ready.

Ed was in the waiting room with Tom Knute. Lucy was there. And Carl Davis. Peter wondered if he had ruined Carl's coat. He hoped not.

He saw Grange. He was skimming along a corridor again and Grange was ahead of him. This place was different. For the technicians off duty. Shops, displays, bright clothes, jewelry. People. They seemed asleep. Moving about, talking, even laughing, but with the unseeing look of somnambulists.

Intersection. A mall on the new street. Trees, grass, beds of flowers: tulips, asters, crocuses, chrysanthemums. He stopped and bent down to touch the grass. Plastic. Plastic flowers from all seasons. Plastic trees. Did they have complete sets of leaves for spring, summer, autumn? Did anyone remember autumn?

There Grange was again. Peter sped after him. Through long assembly lines. Ergs, colorless machine parts, didn't look up as he skimmed along among them. Another room, a mile long, half a mile wide, computer banks. Another section. Labs, cloning labs, prenatal labs, genetic readjustment labs. Machines working, or at rest, being tended carefully by human machines. School rooms. Small Ergs, headsets on, seated before viewing machines, immobile. Exercise yard. In unison: up, down, jump in place, one-two-one-two...

"Grange!"

"You really believe me guilty of gratuitous malevolence?"

The waiter brought two more brandies. "I used to. Not now."

"Well, that's something we can drink to." He did,

deliberately, hardly wetting his tongue. "Ah, Courvoisier. The amenities are vanishing one by one. Thank God, I'll be dead before they're all gone. Ours is the last generation to know such luxuries, you realize?"

"Like the luxury of sunshine and a wind on your face?"

Grange raised his eyebrows but didn't comment. "I have to kill you, Grange. An eye for an eye."

"I was afraid you'd take that attitude. This combination of brilliance and stupidity never fails to amaze me. I gaze on you with awe."

"Meaning?"

"Can you honestly say it isn't better to have all these people alive down here, than dead up there? There would have been crisis after crisis. Military, political, an AEC power plant accident, something that would have started the fires, and once started they would not have been quenchable."

"That wasn't the choice. The choice was to let them go in a different direction without being able to go with them. And you couldn't go with them, could you? Better to force them below ground where control could be absolute. That was the choice."

"Nonsense. Of course, you see it through romantic eyes. Lucy saw that report, my letter to Dunnock. You know what was in it. Everything indicated a catastrophic future. Absolute doom, that's what was in it. That's what lay ahead. I saw how we could save something. And above us the earth is healing itself."

"We're the dinosaurs of this era, Grange."

"That's what I prevented. We'll survive. The race will survive. We saw that it would, we took action while others marched and sang songs and wrung their hands. It's going to be a new era, Peter. In the history books of a distant future you know who they'll celebrate? Me. The Grange era. History will give them the perspective to understand what was at stake, what I did about it. I'm going to do for mankind what evolution would get around to doing in a million years, if we could survive that long. In my lifetime, Peter!"

Peter toyed with his brandy glass. He hadn't drunk any

of it yet, but he was very thirsty. "What will be down here in twenty years? In fifty years? What will be down here in a hundred years?"

"Mankind."

Peter laughed. "This is mankind's grave. We've finally outdone ourselves on a mausoleum."

"Cannula," Krump said and felt the instrument land smartly in his hand. The metal tube had a needle in the end of it, and carefully he inserted it into the taut brain. Right ventricle, he muttered, not out loud. The brain pulsed irregularly, lagging slightly behind the *beep, beep* of the electrocardiogram. No one in the room was unaware of the beeping, no one was unaware that the beeps were too irregular, too slow. Blood pressure was 70 over 50 now. The assistant to the anesthesiologist squeezed the rubber bag, forcing oxygen and the anesthetic into Peter's lungs, and Krump could hear the faint return as Peter exhaled, too faint. Krump allowed no chatter in his operating room, the only voice was his, and his was nearly inaudible most of the time, cursing in a low voice that was raised only to ask for an instrument. He had the ventricle. Slowly he withdrew fluid and the tautness relaxed slightly. Now he could cut, he thought, but slowly, gently. The resident came behind him with the aspirator. "Bovie," Krump said. He extended his hand and the electric scalpel was placed in it, and he resumed his cursing.

Peter searched until he found Carl.

"Carl! Listen. I just realized something. I'm jealous of you, have been from the first time I met you."

"Is that a fact?"

"Especially because of Lucy, of course, but because you made me feel bumbling, dumb, a patsy." Carl was regarding Peter gravely. "We both love her. She has loved both of us. I don't know what I mean."

"A equals B. B equals C. Therefore A equals C?"

"Something like that. Except that A didn't equal C. C was bigger and smarter and more capable." Peter looked at him hard. "But even that isn't all of it. I was jealous because you have something I don't have, don't know how to get. Something to believe in. How do you get it, Carl? Where does it come from?"

Carl's eyes were friendly now, and amused. "There's a lot of roads into Damascus, boy, or didn't you know that?"

"But how do you get on the road?"

In unison they said, "One foot at a time," and they both laughed. Then, sobering again, Peter said, "If I ... Would you take care of her if anything happened?"

Carl laughed again. His teeth were such a shock every time Peter saw them. He exposed so much of them when he laughed and they were so white. And big.

"I'm headed for the pokey, boy, or ain't you heard? Lord knows how many charges they have against me. Everything from theft to conspiracy against the federal government. And you want me to take care of your girl. Who is also going to the pokey, so I hear." He laughed harder. "White boy, you live in a dreamworld."

"Don't mock me, Carl. Answer me. Will you?"

"Yeah, Peter. Yeah."

Peter couldn't hold him. He turned furiously to Krump. "Goddamn you, don't let go yet. Not yet."

Krump aspirated the cut, and now when the grainy tissue was drawn out, he knew it was brain cells. Brain cells in the thalamus, he thought bitterly. What integrative processes was he destroying now? He knew there was no answer to that yet. Not until Peter was awake again. If Peter awakened again. He put his finger into the brain and felt for the mass of abscess. Nothing. Not deep enough. Deeper. Carefully, not in a hurry now. He was functioning with that thing in there, he thought. And it had cut through this same tissue to get inside there. Not like a tumor that grows where it chooses. This was driven there. A bit of helmet. A bone fragment. Something that penetrated this same matter that he now cut into, and that gave him hope. Behind the table the *beep, beep* continued, too irregular, damn it. As if in reply the brain pulsed, but feebly. He felt again. "This is the lamina medullaris medialis," he heard himself muttering. The resident nodded, and the aspirator sucked out grey matter. His fingers would know, Krump thought. They would tell the difference between brain tissue and a pocket of abscess. A slight change in resistance, a hardness in the soft matter, just something not quite right. The fingers would know.

And while that thing, that foreign body with its enveloping pocket of corruption was in there, he thought, what dreams Peter would have have. What nightmares was he experiencing, or what fantasies? He hoped they were pretty fantasies, and feared they were not. No matter. There would be no memory of them afterwards. No matter. But he knew, or thought he knew, that they did matter somehow. Every scene that played in that shadowy theater left a trace of itself, made a difference somehow.

Peter leaned toward Grange, who leaped to his feet. "Don't be a bloody, boring hero," he said in disgust. "You can't appeal to my conscience, because I believe with all my mind that I acted for the best."

"I know you do. That's why I have to kill you." Peter reached for his throat, but Grange eluded him.

This level was given over to services. A hospital. Dispensaries. Storerooms, supplies, convalescent homes, gardens so real looking that Peter almost stepped on the "grass" before its plastic blades became apparent. Grange was seated on a "stone" bench, regarding him.

"Don't be so damned melodramatic. That's the trouble with you young people. You dramatize everything totally beyond recognition. Of course, you can't kill me. You can't even touch me. None of this is real. You are wandering about in my mind and as soon as I go more deeply asleep, or wake up, you'll be gone. Interesting, I'll say then."

Peter laughed this time. Standing before Grange he laughed a long time. "Grange, you're beaten. You don't have to admit it. Its truth doesn't require your acknowledgement."

"Ah, that has a certain ring," Grange said, nodding approval. "Exactly how I would have phrased it. That leaves a dilemma, however. If I fashion you in my image, it shows a certain lack, don't you see? I should be able to reproduce you right down to every bump and wart. You shouldn't talk like me in my dreams."

"Tomorrow the city will start to fade like a dream from the minds of those who are supporting you. Without you to drive them, they'll fold up."

"You are becoming tiresome. You really prefer death for everyone. That's what I find so hard to accept. You'd really stop all progress just like that?"

"No. The only progress that means anything is the progress of the human consciousness, the soul, whatever name you give it, toward its own fulfillment. You don't know enough to recreate man. The golem is your product."

"God, not enough that I conjured you up, you have to lecture like a low-grade moron."

"Watch, Grange, watch while I demolish your city. It's all up here in your head now, and I can rip it apart here. Your city. Your dream. You." Peter played the console of switches, buttons, dials as if it were an organ. A runaway excursion in the atomic generating plant on the lowest level. Another switch sealed all inner doors. Aurora lights from below danced crazily, bursts of red, curtains of orange, yellow flickers. With one quick motion he deactivated the Ergs, those on the assembly lines, in the storage shelves, on the walkways, in the service areas. They all folded up on themselves, dwindled and vanished, leaving small neat piles of ash behind.

Grange lunged toward Peter. "A nightmare," he said hoarsely. "I'm having a nightmare. That's all." He shook his head, then clutched it in pain. "No. Don't. Peter!" He slipped to the floor, on his knees rocking now with pain. "No, Peter, please." And Peter let go, and backed away watching him. No, he thought, not that way. Never again that way.

Lucy was regarding him bitterly. "You could have stopped him! You let him go!"

"Not with magic," Peter said, hoping she could understand, aware that she didn't. "Lucy, there is no magic, only mystery. You don't need to fear mystery."

"I loved you, Peter. Then you went away."

"I love you," he said. She bowed her head and walked away from him. He watched her until she faded into the darkness, and he marked the spot so that he would know where to go to find her again.

In the waiting room Lucy stirred and looked at the high, broad windows with their yellowing shades drawn part way down. If he lived, she thought, then what? She had failed him. She had grown afraid and backed away from him. It was because of his illness, she thought, and bowed her head. It was only because of his illness. No one could truly love a mentally ill person. If he lived, if he recovered, everything would be all right again, the same as it was a long time ago. Someone pressed a paper cup of coffee into her hands and she looked up to see Carl. "He was just sick," she whispered. "Wasn't he, Carl? Just sick."

Carl nodded gravely. "He was very sick," he said, and she wondered at his eyes, which seemed so flat, so unreadable. She glanced at Ed across the room and averted her gaze quickly. How angry, she thought, how afraid, how desperate. She couldn't bear to look at him at all. D. C. stood in the doorway, also looking at Ed. Pale, ill-looking, as desperate as he, she simply watched him, no longer able to go to him, to try to comfort him at all.

"Peter!" D. C. was groping among the ruins, searching for something.

"Come out," he called to her. "This way!"

"I can't. Peter, please stop. Don't you see, I can't leave. The game is all I have. Don't destroy the game too." She was Eurydice, he thought. She knew her last chance was not really a chance at all.

He pushed buttons and walls collapsed. He skimmed up and out of the dust. The sun was low; long golden shafts that looked solid penetrated the spaces between the trees. The ground was cushioned with pine needles. The air was still. No bird sang. Hand in hand he walked with Lucy. Neither of them said anything. There were tears on her cheeks. They glistened when she walked from shade to sunlight. He touched a tear and it was very cool on his finger. It glittered like a diamond on the end of his finger.

In the upper left corner of his room there was a right triangular patch about three inches on its base, about four inches high, that was several shades darker than the walls. The walls were buff-colored.

For a moment Krump thought how his legs ached. His gaze met that of the resident, who would be a great neurosurgeon in his own right one day. The resident shook his head slightly, and his eyes were bleak and filled with the same furious frustration that Krump felt. Where are you now, Peter? Krump thought in despair, and for a moment he thought he was being answered.

"Don't you let go, you Goddamn bastard!" Peter yelled at him from far away, so far away that his voice was lost in the blackness that separated them.

"What they don't understand," Peter said clearly to Krump, moving in very close to him, "is that the sum of the inner explorations is comparable to the discoveries of Magellan and Columbus. Essential, but not totally complete yet. Not totally."

He should close now, or let the resident do it, Krump thought. And he thought, that Goddamned thing had cut through this tissue and Peter had recovered. This was the uncharted sea, where the maps would have you believe dragons dwell, where an injury was death. And Peter had survived. In Japan they had believed there was nothing this deep, because the patient lived; they hadn't probed this deep. No one ever probed this deep unless he knew the patient was a goner anyway. The missile had cut through, he thought again, and a pocket of abscess had formed, and Peter had survived. Krump forgot his legs and visualized the brain stem, that old, old part of the brain whose functions were so imperfectly understood. He was vaguely aware of the resident's quick intake of air as he leaned forward again, and then he forgot him once more.

He deepened the incision. He cursed in a low monotone.

He knew where it had to be. Had to be. A fraction of an inch. His finger felt above, then moved slowly down, up the other side. He stopped and knew he had it. Not very big. Son of a bitch, he muttered, inaudibly, and the resident felt a quickening. Slowly, slowly the Bovie moved now. "Cannula," Krump said and felt it almost instantly. Release the pressure first. Don't want the Goddamn son of a bitch exploding all over the place. But it was not very hard. He drew out a mixture of pus and blood, and when the sac had dwindled somewhat, he withdrew the cannula. Now to open it and clean it out. The *beep, beep* was the only sound. In a minute we'll give you some blood, boy, he promised silently. In a minute.

Peter walked with Krump for a short distance, trying to make him understand. The doctor's shiny head was very pink in the bright light of the place they were in, a place Peter never had been before. "All my life," he said earnestly, "they've been telling me what I can do, what I can't do. They keep telling me that I'm dying, you know." Krump was admiring strange flowers on either side of the walk, his head perspiring, paying no attention to Peter. "No!" Peter yelled at him suddenly. "Just No! Do you understand!" And he thought of the mole under Lucy's breast, how she claimed it was insensitive, but when he kissed her there, how she drew in her breath and her nipples hardened. He thought of the peace under the great trees, and the something he had found there once. He thought of Ed's daughter Bobby, who planned to fish and beachcomb with him for ever and ever. "NO!" Krump continued to walk, admiring the flowers. He picked one, then another, very pleased with them.

Ed sat apart now, a dingy lamp casting dirty light in a circle about him, his eyes deep and hidden in shadows. His face was tight and hard, in a struggle with a terrible rage, a fury so intense that he had forgotten the others.

Ford, he was thinking, that Goddamned, stiff-necked, overrated general. At the meeting Ford had been the only one to insist on Peter's medical detention. Ford had been the one alarmed about what Peter might know, the one who insisted on the interrogation. "Memory is a chemical chain," Grange had said. "You disrupt it, rearrange the components and you have amnesia. After this sort of operation, believe me, my dear General, there is amnesia, and what memories are recovered are not trustworthy. Hasn't that been the case, Senator?" But Ford didn't believe it. And Ed had said, "He's my brother, Ford. Leave it alone." He seethed in the waiting room, hearing over and over Ford's reply, heavy with menace, "Your brother or your neck, Roos!" And now Peter was in there under the knife, and Ford would be safe enough. It was a hit-and-run accident, he repeated to himself. A hit-and-run accident. He wouldn't accept the responsibility. He refused it, denied its existence. *For what*? For Peter. For the war. For Grange. Ford. The arrests. The hit-and-run driver. Especially would he not accept responsibility for the hit-and-run driver. The rage didn't subside.

Peter walked with Lucy under the trees and felt a lifting, soaring something that they couldn't talk about or name, or even mention, for fear of losing it. The tears on Lucy's cheeks glistened as she walked from shade to sunlight. He touched a tear and it was very cool on his finger. It glittered like a diamond on the end of his finger.

The teardrop seemed to grow and Peter felt that he was moving away from it with incredible acceleration, faster and faster, and still the drop grew, and now it took on color; it was the world, the way the world looked in the astronauts' photographs. Very beautiful. And he was leaving it farther and farther behind him until it reached its full size and rapidly began to dwindle again. The colors faded from it until it glistened like a star and again he thought, how beautiful it was. All of it. And somewhere a door closed.

Beep. Krump didn't tense, but he listened for the second one, and when it finally came, he knew that although not a muscle had stiffened, something in him had. He finished cleaning out the pocket of the abscess, taking care to be scrupulous now. They would peer at the matter through microscopes and they would sort out the foreign object and put a name to it, and they would be able to label this as a case of such-and-such embedded in the right thalamus, and on paper it would look so simple. "Blood," he said, and the i.v. started a flow of blood. Now they would close. The resident should close. Good practice for him. Krump thought how his legs ached and nodded to the resident. He tried not to look as if the resident might butcher his child, and now he handled the aspirator and kept his hands out of the way. He listened to the *beep, beep*, and thought that it was steadier, but he didn't ask what the pressure was. Not yet.

With the closing of the door Peter felt himself being propelled back. An impossible orbit, he thought with interest. A hyperbolic orbit, and he simply had stopped and reversed, and now was on a collision course with that speck that glistened in the darkness. The race back was exhilarating, and he felt a freedom and joy that he could not restrain. Laughing, he yelled one long sustained cry of triumph, and the "Whoooeee!" streamed out behind him filling the blackness. Then he slept without dreams.

The anesthesiologist adjusted his dials, giving Peter plain oxygen now. A nurse counted her cottonoids. Another nurse assisted with the bandaging, and Krump stepped back, remaining for only a moment longer. "We did it, boy," he said softly.

And Peter slept.

The long-awaited new adventure by the
greatest writing team in science fiction—

OVER 3 MILLION OF THEIR BOOKS IN PRINT!

LARRY NIVEN
and
JERRY POURNELLE!

OATH
of
FEALTY

A gripping epic of a near-future America, of a high-
technology Utopia rising above the ruins of Los
Angeles—and its desperate struggle to survive the
awesome forces that surround it!

The authors of **The Mote in God's Eye, Inferno** and
Lucifer's Hammer surpass the excitement and
suspense of their earlier books in a novel that will leave
you breathless!

POCKET BOOKS

472